One of the Guys

Book 5 of the *Love Unexpected* series

Delaney Diamond

Chapter One

The bright sunny day contrasted in the extreme to Ronnie's dark mood.

Months ago, she promised herself to steer clear of blind dates and setups. They always ended in disaster. Yet somehow her well-meaning, meddling cousin Anika missed the memo and invited Ronnie to Shula's for dinner and drinks, all the while planning a setup.

Ronnie should have known something was up when Anika suggested—multiple times during the initial phone call—that she wear a dress and "put on a little makeup." They'd barely sat down when Anika's coworker, Edgar, just happened to run into them and, upon her cousin's insistence, joined them for dinner.

As expected, the night ended miserably. Edgar's car wouldn't start. Luckily, instead of her father's car, Ronnie drove her pickup, her vehicle of preference. She loved her baby and rebuilt the engine herself.

After diagnosing the problem, she pulled out her toolbox and went to work, right there in the parking lot of the restaurant. Dirt and grease stains soiled the red shirt-dress she wore, but a grateful Edgar was able to drive his car home.

Ronnie slammed the door of her older model blue Nissan 4 X 4 and trudged up the driveway to the two-story red brick house she shared with her father. The scent of freshly cut grass filled her nose from her neighbor's yard. Five years in a row, Dr. Reynolds, the professor who lived next door, had won the homeowners association's beautification award. Not only because he kept his bright green grass cut low, but because the giant hydrangea bushes on the street side of his fence burst with purple color and added charm to the quiet block.

"Hey there, Ronnie." The professor waved from the sidewalk, his brown and white Shih Tzu strutting along ahead of him with her nose in the air.

Ronnie waved back. "Good morning, Dr. Reynolds."

The automatic reference to the time of day caused her to glance at her watch, and she grimaced at the lateness of the hour. Eleven thirty, half the day gone already, and she still needed a shower and change of clothes before going to work.

She smiled at the early blooms of the Knock Out Roses her father planted in the fall, and made a mental note to tell him to trim back the bushes.

Quiet greeted her when she entered the house. Her father must have left for the grocery store already. The soft soles of her cross-strap flats hardly made a sound on the old cherry hardwood floor when she eased by the table and oval mirror in the entryway.

"Do you know what time it is?" Ezekiel Taylor's gravelly voice filled the air.

Ronnie winced at the disapproval in his tone. Without turning around, she greeted her father. "Good morning, Daddy."

"Good morning? It's almost noon." Clearly he was in a foul mood.

She sighed and plastered a smile on her face before turning to face her father's wrath. "It's still morning, though."

At five foot six, Ezekiel was only four inches taller than his daughter, with a stocky but firm build. His skin, a shade lighter than hers, was back to its brilliant glow, when only a few days ago he'd had an unhealthy gray pallor during his recovery from a bout with pneumonia.

Her father spoke gruffly, but she never paid him any mind. People who didn't know him well thought he was rude, but she was accustomed to his tone.

"I brought you lunch." She held up the bag, a peace offering she had the foresight to pick up on the way home.

He hesitated, mouth open, apparently considering whether or not to lambast her again, and then decided to go for it. "You think you can sweet-talk me with food?"

It's worked before, Ronnie thought. "Of course not."

Sighing, she continued to the kitchen, with her father hot on her heels, and deposited the paper sack on the counter.

"You need to call when you stay out all night."

"Come on, Daddy, I'm grown."

"I still worry, nugget," he snapped.

"Dang, I'm sorry. It won't happen again."

There were plenty of benefits to living at home. For instance, she always had company, and her living expenses were a fraction of what they'd be if she lived alone. The big drawback, however, was being a twenty-six-year-old woman, but treated like a twelve-year-old child.

"What kind of nonsense did Anika get you into this time?"

Ronnie washed her hands at the sink. "Nothing much. We hung out at Shula's and she introduced me to one of her co-workers. A guy named Edgar."

"Did you like him?"

"He was okay. Might be cool to hang out with some time." She liked Edgar's even-tempered personality, and he knew a lot about sports, one of her favorite topics of discussion. She removed the po'boy sandwich she bought for herself.

Ezekiel let out a heavy sigh. "I don't understand young people nowadays. Do y'all ever date? You're always 'hanging out' or 'talking' or 'hooking up.'"

"What do you know about hooking up?" Ronnie asked, amused. She rested a fist on her hip.

"I know plenty. Whatever happened to courting?"

"I'm pretty sure it went out with the horse and buggy," Ronnie deadpanned.

Ezekiel's lips flattened into a line of disapproval, and she grinned at him. She shouldn't get so much pleasure from teasing her father.

"That's not how we do things nowadays." Ideally she wanted a meaningful relationship, but until then was perfectly fine "hanging out."

"Just because that's how you do things, don't make it right. In my day, you courted, and a young man showed respect by meeting a young woman's parents. That's the way your mama and I did it."

Ronnie couldn't remember anything about her

mother, though she wished she could. Rosie Taylor passed away twenty-four years ago. Photos scattered around the house kept her memory alive—a large framed photo over the fireplace mantel, pictures of her in the albums in the den, and a small picture of her and Ezekiel sitting on the wall at Niagara Falls during the second day of their honeymoon. As far as her father was concerned, her mother might as well have died last week. He'd never stopped pining for her.

"Times have changed. People have evolved. Guess what? Women approach men nowadays. And they like it. Gasp." She widened her eyes for good measure.

"One of these days, love's gonna knock you on that narrow little ass of yours, and we'll see how cocky you are then."

Ronnie laughed at the prediction, one he'd leveled at her before. "Thank you for the warning. Did you take your medicine?" If she didn't stay on him, he'd forget.

He tugged the collar of his robe. "Of course I took my medicine. I feel much better, but I know the doctor said to finish the prescription."

"That's right." She pulled the second meal from the bag. "I brought your favorite from the place down on Candler Street. Catfish, French fries, and hush puppies." Once a week she let him have fried food, but suspected he cheated when she wasn't around.

"Did you remember my hot sauce?" Ezekiel asked.

"Yes Daddy, I remembered your hot sauce," Ronnie answered, rolling her eyes. She'd forgotten one time. One time, and he never let her forget it.

"Good." Ezekiel slathered tartar sauce and hot

sauce on his catfish. "What happened to your dress?"

"I ended up under the hood of Edgar's car."

She told him the whole story, right down to the end when Edgar begged her to take some money but she refused. Her father listened attentively, stuffing fries into his mouth like they were an endangered food item.

"Afterward, I was tired and it was late, so I spent the night at Anika's."

"Remember to call next time."

"I will."

"How are things down at the shop?"

"Okay," Ronnie answered, though the situation was anything but. Business at Taylor Automotive & Repair had slowed in recent months, but she didn't want to bother him with her concerns. She'd think of a creative way to boost revenue soon.

"You still having trouble with Diego?" her father asked. He placed a morsel of catfish in his mouth.

At the mention of her Cuban business neighbor, a knot formed in her belly and her fingers tightened on her sandwich. Her father knew of him but had never met him.

"I've got it under control."

Diego owned the towing company housed in the building right next door to the auto shop. Ever since he moved in, he'd been nothing but a pain in the ass. She wished he'd never bought the business from the previous owner.

"Let me know if you want me to step in. If you continue to have trouble, you can always talk to the landlord."

"I know."

Ezekiel grunted. "This is good catfish."

They ate in silence for a while, standing at the counter, both enjoying their individual meals.

Chewing slowly, Ronnie studied the surroundings with critical eyes. The kitchen could use some updating. New tile to replace the linoleum, and white cabinets with new fixtures could really spruce up the space. She'd change out the lighting, too, and replace the single overhead with a row of recessed lights to brighten the room. The green stove and wall oven, which she assumed were the original, performed their functions well, but needed to be replaced with modern appliances.

Unfortunately, business at the shop had fallen off so much, she couldn't make the updates she'd like to, and renovating the kitchen represented nothing more than an unattainable goal.

"You going out again tonight?" Her father dabbed his mouth with a napkin.

"I may go to the sports bar later. Would you rather I stay with you?" If he said yes, she'd stay and keep him company.

Ever since her mother died, it had just been the two of them. She could have long ago moved out and rented her own place but couldn't fathom leaving her father behind to fend for himself. Especially not now. He lacked the energy he used to have, and a few years ago quit working as a mechanic at Taylor Automotive—his only other pride and joy besides her. He preferred to stay busy, though, and volunteered his time at Sumpter Technical College, offering advice to the students on track to become auto technicians.

Ezekiel shook his head. "You don't have to stay with me. I'm going over to Davis's house tonight for some bachelor party fun," he said, referring to one of the deacons from church. "Can you believe him, getting married to a young thing like that, at his age?"

The "young thing" was a woman in her early forties, but being that Davis was in his late sixties, the twenty-five-year difference raised eyebrows.

"If you weren't so ornery, maybe you could find a young thing," Ronnie said. She popped a fried shrimp from the sandwich into her mouth.

He guffawed. "In five more years, I'll be seventy, girl. Ain't no woman gonna date an old fart like me."

"Davis is around your age," Ronnie pointed out.

Ezekiel brushed aside her argument with a wave of his hand. "I've got way more problems than Davis. My eyes are bad and my bones creak, and ain't no woman good enough to take your mama's place, no way."

Her heart twinged at the offhand comment. Staring at what was left of her sandwich, Ronnie thought how her father had doomed himself to a life of loneliness. The stubborn old man refused to let anyone else in. Several of the matrons at church were interested in him, but he paid them no mind, and the single widow next door—Miss Loretta—obviously liked him too, but he paid no attention to her.

Ezekiel gathered his meal and took a can of soda from the refrigerator. "You going in to the shop?"

"In a little bit, after I eat and take a shower."

"All right. I may not see you until tomorrow, since I'll be at Davis's." He headed out the kitchen.

"Don't party too hard," Ronnie called.

His only response was a grunt.

She watched his retreating back in his ratty navy-blue and white bathrobe—where the blue had faded to powder blue and the white edged toward gray. He'd had the thing for years, and she once accused him of being cheap and threw out the robe and bought him a new one. To her dismay, he retrieved it from the trash and insisted it was still perfectly fine. Only later did she learn it was the last gift her mother gave him. She took the purchase back to the store for a refund the very next day.

Ronnie leaned her pelvis against the counter and stared out the window, Miss Loretta's yard in her immediate line of vision. The older woman was locking up and glancing over at the house, saw Ronnie. They waved at each other and then Miss Loretta shuffled to the dark sedan parked in the driveway.

On occasion, she came over carrying a delicious pie or cake, claiming she made them to stay busy and couldn't finish them all. The poor woman always looked all googly-eyed at Ezekiel, smiling hopefully every time she handed over one of the desserts. All she received for her trouble was a brief thank you when Ronnie returned the empty dish.

Ronnie tossed the paper sack and the cellophane from her sandwich into the trash.

She suspected her father and Miss Loretta would make a perfect match. How sad some people couldn't see what was right there in front of them.

Chapter Two

Diego Molina frustrated her.

Arms crossed over her chest, Ronnie tapped her foot, watching from the empty waiting room of the shop as he parked his flatbed truck across multiple spaces in the lot they shared, a gray Volkswagen Jetta sitting on top of it. For the hundred thousandth time she'd have to remind him not to park across the premium parking spaces reserved for the customers.

He came around from the driver's side. She stopped tapping and just watched him.

Six feet tall and built like a powerhouse, Diego Molina was one of the finest men she'd ever seen, with a head full of luxurious black locks and sage-green eyes that stood out against the dusky complexion of his face. He moved with quiet confidence, the loose-fitting jeans unable to hide the powerful muscles of his thighs and a firm behind. His tan work shirt had to be a polyester blend, yet managed to mold to his broad chest like spandex. The short sleeves exposed tan arms, sprinkled with hair and muscular from the biceps down to the wrists.

Ronnie worked with men and hung out with them all the time. Lots of men. But something about him was more masculine than other men she interacted with.

He made her flesh prickle. Her heart race. And, though she didn't want to admit it, even to herself, had twice or thrice invaded her subconscious through hot sex dreams that startled her awake, nipples aching, body throbbing.

Shaking off her musings, Ronnie stepped into the sun, but stopped in the middle of the lot when Diego opened the door of the passenger side of his truck. He placed a hand on the elbow of the woman in the seat and helped her to the ground.

"Thank you so much. You've been an absolute doll and such a gentleman," she gushed. She tossed her blonde hair and batted her eyelashes at him.

"Just doing my job," Diego said, his accented voice carrying a trace of his Cuban heritage.

"Well, I appreciate it." The woman ran a hand over his bare arm, as if she couldn't help herself.

Ronnie rolled her eyes. Perhaps she shouldn't be too hard on the woman. Four-inch heels and a tight skirt could prove problematic when descending from a truck that high, but running a hand down his arm was clearly inappropriate.

Of course she'd seen this same scenario play out numerous times before, with only slight variances in the action.

Diego cast his lazy gaze on a woman. They swooned and gushed and giggled.

On occasion he'd turned the same smoldering gaze

on Ronnie, but unlike Madame Touchy-Feely, she knew better than to fall prey to all that testosterone-oozing charm.

"Just the person I wanted to see," Diego said, looking at Ronnie. His customer also cast a glance in her direction. He led the blonde over. "This is the owner of Taylor Automotive, and she can fix you right up."

"Her?" she said, eyes widening.

"Hello." Ronnie smiled, hoping her face wasn't as tight as it felt. With less than ten percent of mechanics being women, she somewhat understood why people were surprised when they saw her, but the reaction grated more when it came from a woman.

Behind the customer, Diego did a poor job of hiding a smile behind his knuckles.

"What seems to be the problem?" Ronnie asked.

"Er, well…"

The woman glanced at Diego for approval. He nodded, silently prodding her to go into detail. Ronnie kept the smile on her face and waited. After years of working as an auto tech, she had mastered the art of keeping her cool with her customers. Men tested her, asking trick questions to trip her up, and women doubted her abilities. Sooner or later she won them over with her patience and knowledge.

"For the past…I don't know…week or so, my car has been making a horrible squealing noise."

"When you start it or when you accelerate?"

Using probing questions, Ronnie eased the information from the customer. By the end of the conversation, the blonde smiled, visibly relaxed, and confirmed trust shifted in Ronnie's favor when she asked, "You think you can fix it?"

"We'll do our best," Ronnie said, though based on the answers, she assumed the problem was a routine but costly timing belt but needed to get under the hood to be sure. Pointing at the storefront, she said, "If you go inside, Alfred will get you entered into the system. He's a certified master VW mechanic, so I'm confident we can figure out the problem."

She placed a reassuring hand on the woman's forearm and was rewarded with a smile of relief.

"Thank you!" Ms. Touchy-Feely shot another glance and smile at Diego, who stood silently by watching the exchange, before she hustled into the shop.

"Good job," Diego said.

"I need to talk to you."

He groaned and let his head fall back. "What do you want to complain about today, Veronica Pain-In-My-Ass Taylor?" He stuck a toothpick in his mouth and folded his arms over his chest.

She dragged her eyes from the way his muscles bulged into more prominence.

"Haha, very funny." Pressing her hands onto her narrow hips, Ronnie glared at him. "Why do you always have to park your truck like that and take up the limited parking available for customers?"

"Is that what I did?" He scanned the almost empty parking lot they shared, chewing on the toothpick so it bobbed up and down between his full lips.

"You know good and well that's what you did. I've told you plenty of times before. Since you bought this place, you've created a mess. You take up extra parking spaces, you block my garage bays—"

"Only when they're empty," he pointed out.

"You have no right to do that! Your guys leave

trash in the back lot, and when are you going to move all those abandoned cars?"

At least ten cars sat in the fenced lot at the back of the buildings that hadn't been picked up by their owners, and he appeared in no hurry to get rid of them.

"Let me handle my business, and you handle yours."

"I try to handle mine, but as you can see"—she made a broad, sweeping gesture to showcase the lot—"someone doesn't understand how to be a good neighbor."

He tossed the toothpick to the ground and narrowed his eyes on her. "Are you the one leaving bad reviews for my business online?"

"Of course not!" The accusation stung. Not only was it unethical, her business and his were intertwined. She benefited if he did well.

Diego didn't only bring her customers. He used Taylor Automotive to fix up cars he'd towed that were abandoned by their owners, and he in turn sold them for a profit. From what she could tell, that was a nice side business in addition to the towing company.

"I would be disappointed in you if you did." Diego came closer and she held her breath. Dropping his voice, he said, "However, your whining and bitching is getting out of hand."

"Under the circumstances, I'm very calm."

"I've seen calm, and you're not it. I've told you before I could fix you up and knock that bad attitude right out of you."

"First of all, I don't have a bad attitude." Except with him. He provoked the worst in her. "Second of all, I thought I made myself clear that you're not my type."

"You've never tried my type."

"How do you know what I've tried?" Ronnie asked, knowing she entered dangerous waters with the direction of the conversation, but unable to stop the slide into the unknown.

He sucked air between his teeth. "*Ay no*, you've never been with a Cuban man, *mami*. That much I know. It will change your whole life. You know what they say, once you go Cuban, you never go back." He chuckled to himself, rubbing a hand over his shirt, and she couldn't help but notice his massive hands and broad chest.

"That's not the saying."

"It is now." His voice was low when he spoke next. "I keep telling you, a little horizontal salsa will do you some good."

The air squeezed from her lungs and Ronnie's chest tightened. She took a quivering breath. "I promise you, that will never happen," she said, in her coolest voice possible.

The lids of his eyes lowered over his pupils as he did a lazy scan of her body. The brazen inspection made her feel uncomfortable in her own skin. A sensation, light and airy like a shadow, crept over her, compelling the hairs on her neck to stand on end.

"Oh, *mami*, you don't know what you're missing."

"Not even if pigs fly and hell freezes over." Icicles dripped from her voice.

"So that's a maybe?"

She laughed a little. If there was one thing she could say about Diego, he was consistent. For over a year she'd had to deal with his lascivious smile and cavalier attitude. No matter how many times she shot him down, he came right back with a new line.

"That's a never." She moved closer to him and stood on tiptoe to get in his face, their heads mere inches apart. She made her face into a mask of sweetness and lowered her voice to a seductive purr. "Stop parking your damn truck in the customer parking spaces or I'm calling the landlord." She often threatened to sic the landlord on him but never actually had.

He moaned and shivered, like a man who'd experienced something so exquisite he could barely stand it. "Oh Veronica, I love it when you talk dirty to me."

Diego dropped his eyes to her chest, but this time the brazen inspection didn't only fill her with unease. Heat burned her cheeks, and her traitorous breasts tightened in excitement at the attention. Fortunately, he couldn't see their reaction under the loose-fitting gray overalls.

Ronnie curled her fingers into fists. There was no getting through to him. "Ugh!"

She swung around and stormed away. Yanking open the door, she hurried inside her shop. The sound of his amused laughter only disappeared when the door finally closed behind her.

Chapter Three

"She looks like she wants to kill you. Who was that?" The question came from Dave, the African-American driver Diego hired only days ago. He'd pulled up a few minutes before and walked toward Diego.

"Ronnie Taylor. She runs the mechanic shop," Diego answered.

"She's not a fan of yours," his employee pointed out.

"Seems that way," Diego muttered.

He couldn't figure Ronnie out. He never suffered from a shortage of female company, and for years had been able to get just about any woman he wanted. That wasn't arrogance. It was simply the truth.

As a teen, he dated a congressman's daughter, much to the dismay of her parents. His last relationship was with a wealthy older woman thirteen years his senior who offered a car and apartment to continue the relationship. A month ago, a few well-

placed words and the flash of a smile helped him
avoid a speeding ticket, and he ended the night
playing a sexy new version of cops and robbers with a
particularly frisky female officer.

So why couldn't he get through to Ronnie?

Her constant rebuffs only made him try harder
because he couldn't get her out of his head. Her full,
lush lips were the kind of lips that were not only
perfect for kissing, but perfect for other more wicked
acts. She never wore jewelry and except for the
occasional lip gloss, makeup never graced her dark,
bistre-brown complexion. But by the silky-smooth
appearance of her skin, she didn't need it.

She had what some might consider a masculine
haircut, her natural hair cut low on her head and only
allowed to grow an inch or so before she cut it all off
again, but the haircut brought attention to her eyes.
They were gorgeous, large, luminous—earthy brown,
like soil, and with a curtain of thick lashes.

The hideous gray of the mechanic's overalls
couldn't detract from the brown of her skin, which
was like a blank canvas, open to a palette of colors.
The loose-fitting jumpsuit hinted at her slender
curves and made him more curious about what lay
beneath. If he had his way, he'd know exactly what
her naked body looked like and felt like a long time
ago.

Diego's phone rang and he fished it out of his
pocket. He immediately recognized the number. Loisa
Jimenez was someone whose call he always answered.

"Do me a favor." He tossed Dave the keys to his
truck. "Take down the VW, and move the truck to
the back lot."

"Sure thing."

One of the Guys

Heading toward the unremarkable tan building that housed his towing company, Diego answered the call. "¿*Oigo*?"

The female voice on the other end continued the conversation in Spanish. "Hi. Do you have a few minutes to talk?"

"I always have time for you. You know that."

She laughed, the sound of her laughter still one of her best features. During the period they shared an apartment and planned a life together, her laughter and good humor had been an aspect he looked forward to on a daily basis, particularly during the darkest period of his life.

"You always say the sweetest things," she said.

"I mean it."

Ambling into the tiled waiting area, he nodded at Rosita behind the counter, who worked the day shift as a receptionist and dispatcher. The property was along a fairly busy road during the day, but at night traffic slowed to a trickle, so for second shift Diego preferred a male dispatcher who brought along his Rottweiler, Demon, to keep him company.

He closed the door to his office, a small square dominated by an old metal desk covered by a wooden top, inherited from the previous owner and filled with work orders, bills, and miscellaneous other documents that needed his review. He hated the paperwork but took pride in running his own company, a feat he'd never imagined accomplishing at the age of twenty-eight.

Fortunately, a little over a year ago and two years into his move to Atlanta, the previous owner of this establishment was in a financial bind and on the verge of bankruptcy when the opportunity presented itself for him to become a business owner. After negotiating owner financing and a small down payment, he took over the towing company and renamed it D&M Towing. He inherited six drivers and two dispatchers.

As luck would have it, being next door to the mechanic shop facilitated a worthwhile side business. Whenever he towed junk cars or owners abandoned their towed vehicles, he could apply for title and sell them to a scrap yard. He let Taylor Automotive fix the better ones, and he sold them for a tidy little profit.

He set his booted feet on the desk and crossed them at the ankles. "What's going on with you?"

"Well, I need to ask you a big favor," Loisa said slowly.

The hesitancy in her voice aroused his curiosity, but he wanted to assure her that whatever she needed she could have. "Anything," he said.

"I was hoping you'd say that. Here's the thing: I'm moving to Atlanta in the fall, and I was hoping I could stay at your place while I look around for an apartment."

The request took him by surprise, and his relaxed body tensed.

She laughed softly. "Don't worry, Diego, I'm not going to try to seduce you. Our relationship is over, and I accept my role in making that happen."

He'd loved her desperately at one time, but Loisa cheated on him. As far as he was concerned, he'd pushed her into the arms of another man, yet he couldn't and didn't look at her the same way after the affair. But they worked through it and became friends, linked by a past filled with equal parts joy and pain.

"I just need a place to stay while I'm in Atlanta looking around. My job is transferring me there, and it'll be cheaper than staying in a hotel. I hope that's okay with you."

"I can't believe you're leaving Miami."

She'd lived there all her life. Her family resided there. For her to move was not only shocking, it was a drastic change.

"A position opened up in Atlanta. I applied and got it. I have to wrap up here, but I want to get a head start on nailing down living arrangements. The company is paying for me to move, but not for me to come there and look around at my own leisure. Since you're there…well, I figured I could take advantage and stay at your place for a few days while I look around."

Loisa worked as an analyst for a financial services firm based in Florida, but with offices throughout the United States.

"That's not a problem at all," Diego said.

"I won't be cramping your style, will I?"

"Now you're fishing for information," he said, his mouth quirking up in the corner.

"I *am* fishing a little bit," she admitted. "But not for the reason you think. I don't want to cause any problems."

"You're staying, what, a few days? It won't be a problem. When are you thinking about coming?"

She gave him a date and Diego made a mental note.

"That works for me. I'll make sure I'm available to take you around if you need me to."

"Thank you. I knew I could count on you."

She went quiet, and in the weighted silence he knew there was more she wanted to say.

"What are you doing for the Anniversary this year?" she asked in a soft, hesitant voice.

His abdomen tightened.

The Anniversary. A date that arrived every year and reminded him of the beginning of the most painful part of their relationship. The day their daughter passed away.

He swallowed the lump in his throat.

"Are you there?" Loisa asked quietly.

"I'm here," he answered hoarsely.

"I didn't mean to upset you. I—"

"You didn't upset me." He rubbed his fingers across his brow to alleviate the gentle throbbing that emerged. "I usually spend the Anniversary alone." Except for last year, when he went to his cousin's house in the country for a few days.

"Me, too." She sighed. "She would be eight this year. Our baby would be eight."

Pain and loss vibrated in her voice, and he wasn't in the frame of mind to handle the riot of emotion talking about their daughter evoked.

He dropped his feet to the floor. "I should go. I'll call you in a few weeks, or you call me and we'll make definitive plans. I need to finish up some work."

"Of course you do. I'm so sorry. I know that you're busy. Have a good day, Diego. We'll talk again in a few weeks."

Diego hung up in a rush and dropped his phone to the desk. He rested his elbows on his knees and supported his head on his fists. Closing his eyes, he breathed slowly in and out, forcing calm into his spirit.

He'd prided himself on being the opposite of his own father, a monster who never offered love or affection. Only alcoholic rages that resulted in vitriolic rants and emotional and physical pain.

The image of his little girl came back to him. Matilda, with her honey-brown skin, closer to her mother's complexion. She'd been the light of his life, and for three years he'd been lucky enough to call himself her father. Her protector. Her champion.

He'd been at work and, when he received the call, was certain they'd made a mistake. But there was no mistake. He and Loisa arrived at the hospital together, and his Matilda was gone. Loisa collapsed, and except for the streaks of tears that escaped his eyes, Diego went numb.

That numbness lasted for two years. He fell into an abyss, a dark place where no one could reach him.

He pulled out his wallet and stared at the picture of Matilda, three years old with her dark hair in pigtails and grinning at the camera. He smiled slightly and ran a calloused finger over the image of her sweet face.

When his baby girl died that day, she took a big chunk of his heart, his soul, and his sanity.

Moving to Atlanta had been good for him. His cousin Tomas lived here, and the city contained a thriving, close-knit Cuban community. But to this day he still felt an emptiness in his heart he was certain could never be filled again.

Chapter Four

Ronnie spent Monday morning ordering parts and then finished a transmission rebuild on a newer-model vehicle she had started on Friday. She ate lunch with Alfred, an old white man with silvery white hair, craggy eyebrows, and surprisingly bright eyes in a pale, wrinkled face. He'd worked with her father for many years and his knowledge and experience proved invaluable when she took over running the shop.

They went over the schedule in her office, a small space that two months ago she spent an afternoon painting white. Invoices and notices were pinned to the walls, and spare parts and batteries piled on top of wire shelves that surrounded the eight-foot table she used as a desk.

She currently employed three full-time mechanics, two part-time mechanics, and a weekend office manager, a young man in his early twenties earning extra money while he attended school to earn an automotive service technology certificate.

At the end of the lunch meeting, Ronnie sent home one of the part-timers and one of the full-time employees. If by some chance a couple of unscheduled customers came through the doors before closing, she was confident she, Alfred, and the other two techs could handle the repairs.

She was about to do an oil change on a Lexus for a customer who would return after work to retrieve it, when she heard a bouncing basketball and hollering men. The sounds penetrated the noise of tools and Alfred singing along to a country music song playing on the portable radio in his service area.

Diego had installed a basketball net last year to give his men an outlet during slow periods. Ronnie went to stand in the open doorway and watched him and Dave, whom he recently hired, and Justin, a wiry white guy with a waist-length ponytail, roughhousing and grunting as they ran around.

Justin grabbed the rebound and spotted Ronnie. "We have an audience," he announced. Using a graceful fadeaway, he shot the ball clean through the net. Grinning, he winked at her.

Justin tended to flirt, but not as much as Diego. Once or twice he made a comment about taking her out and asked if she ever considered trying "white chocolate." She completely ignored him, considering he was getting married in the fall.

Ronnie leaned a shoulder against the door and pointed at the food wrappers piled along the back wall. "Are you guys going to clean up this mess when you're finished?" she asked.

"Don't we always?" Diego asked. He dribbled the ball and hustled away from Dave.

"No, you don't, actually. The lot is a pigsty."

"*Dios, mami*, do anything but complaints ever come from that gorgeous mouth of yours?"

Gorgeous mouth. The compliment sent heat radiating through her body.

Diego shot the ball and missed. "Look what you made me do," he said.

"I didn't make you do that."

He sauntered over, and Ronnie straightened, stuffing her hands in her pockets.

"Diego, you finished?" Dave asked.

"I'll be back in a minute," he called, not taking his eyes off Ronnie.

The men continued playing, while she Diego continued their staring contest.

"Why do you have such a problem with me?" he asked.

"You really have to ask? You act as if you're the only one leasing this space. My business is here, too, and the condition of the property affects me."

"No one comes in the back lot. You just want to give me a hard time."

"Believe me, I get no pleasure out of always having to be the bad guy."

"I think you get a lot of pleasure out of it."

A sexy smile crossed his lips, making her toes curl in her comfortable black lace-ups. Every time he spoke, his voice sounded low and enticing, almost dirty.

"Well, you're wrong," Ronnie said.

"From the beginning you've been rude to me," Diego said, pointing a finger at her.

"What are you talking about?"

"From the first day when my office was closed and

you didn't accept that package. Instead, you sent the UPS man on his way."

She remembered the day well, and didn't know why she didn't accept the package. She never hesitated to do small favors like that for the previous owner. "You stormed over to my shop and yelled at me. I'm not your secretary."

"No, but you're my neighbor. Would it have killed you to be nice?"

"Would it have killed you to show a little respect?" Ronnie shot back with attitude, getting up on her toes.

They both took deep breaths, tempers flaring at the past transgressions.

"You know what, forget it." He waved his hand. "One of these days I'll find a way to shut you up."

"Empty threats don't bother me. The only way to shut me up is to do what you're *supposed* to do," Ronnie said in an extra-sweet voice. She received unprecedented pleasure out of needling him.

"You're a control freak." Diego shook his head and strutted away.

"Of course, there's another way you can shut me up."

He stopped and slowly turned around. Behind him, Justin and Dave continued to grunt and shove each other in their particularly intense game.

"I'm listening," Diego said, eyes narrowed.

Ronnie ambled forward. "Why don't we play a game? If I win, you keep the property clean, file for the abandoned vehicles, and park your trucks where they should go—not in prime customer parking spots. If you win, I'll leave you alone. Shut my mouth from now on."

He stroked his jaw. "What game are we talking about?"

"How about...basketball?" Ronnie said, as if the idea came to her out of the blue.

"Basketball?" Diego smirked.

"Yes. I challenge you to a game of basketball." Ronnie lifted her chin.

Diego snorted. "Are you serious? I'm six feet tall. You're what...five feet?"

"Five two," Ronnie corrected firmly, standing erect.

"Same difference." Diego shrugged.

"No, it's not. But whatever. Do we have a deal?"

He stepped closer and her chest tightened. "I play basketball every weekend at a gym. You really want to do this?"

"Yes."

"Okay, in that case, I want to add one more thing." His gaze flicked over her. Brazen. Indecent. A flush of heat covered her neck and cheeks. "In addition to keeping your mouth shut, if I win, you wear a dress to work."

"A dress? That's not practical."

"Those are my terms." Diego made a careless shrug.

She hesitated.

"Fine, if you win, I'll wear a dress to work," Ronnie said, lips tight. "We'll play tonight, after closing."

"Perfect." He walked off, chuckling. "Can't wait to see those legs."

"Cocky bastard," she muttered.

"I heard that."

"I wanted you to," she flung over her shoulder,

inflecting her voice with annoyance.

But she was smiling to herself.

****

Ronnie stretched, gearing up for the match against Diego. She rolled her neck, watching him chat idly with three of his men, completely unconcerned about the forthcoming game.

D&M Towing and Taylor Automotive & Repair had already closed for the evening. The mechanics and tow truck drivers gathered around the basketball hoop for the big game between the bosses.

The evening air was perfect for a basketball game, cool with a gentle breeze. The lights were already turned on to illuminate the parking lot.

"All right, let's do this," Alfred said, playing the part of referee by holding the basketball aloft.

Ronnie and Diego approached each other. Ronnie rolled her neck and made eye contact with Diego. He appeared amused, unperturbed by her competitive nature.

"I want a clean match," Alfred said, and stated the rules. He concluded with, "First one to ten wins."

They flipped a coin. Ronnie took the ball, and the gathered men immediately began cheering for their individual employers.

Ronnie edged toward the basket, but Diego blocked her with arms spread wide. However, with quick footwork and a cross over, she shifted direction and went around him, hit the layup, and the ball went in. Nothing but net.

On the sidelines, the mechanics cheered and pumped their fists.

"Yeah! Go ahead, Ronnie!"

Diego took the ball next, dribbling toward the

hoop. He eyed her with caution, the humor gone from his face. He clearly recognized that misjudging her because of her height had been a mistake.

While he was bouncing the ball, Ronnie darted at him, stole it, and ran several feet away. With a quick turn, she faded back and tossed it in. Swoosh! Nothing but net.

More yelling from the sidelines.

"Come on, Diego! You got this, boss," Dave called, although he didn't sound quite as convinced as his words.

Diego grabbed the ball and stared at her, breathing hard, finally realizing he was outmatched. He dribbled again and Ronnie stripped away the ball. Diego gaped at her, his eyebrows coming down over his eyes.

Ronnie smirked at him. "Did I mention I played varsity basketball in high school? And for two years in a row I led the state in three-pointers." Standing way back, Ronnie lined up the shot and tossed the ball into the basket.

Nothing but net.

More shouts from the men filled the night air.

The game wrapped up shortly thereafter, the final score of two to ten, in favor of Ronnie.

The mechanics filed back toward the building, with words of "Good game," and "Way to go, boss."

Diego's men sauntered off with much less enthusiasm.

"Hey, you tried," Justin said.

Dave patted his shoulder.

When they were alone, Ronnie tossed the ball at Diego, and he automatically caught it.

"Don't feel bad," she said. "All you have to do is be a good neighbor. Like I said, I'm only asking you to do what you're supposed to do."

She sauntered away, an extra swagger in her step.

"It's not over." His words sounded like a threat.

She glanced over her shoulder. "It is over."

"No." He shook his head. "You can't run forever, *mami*."

Heat prickled her skin in the cool air. "What's that supposed to mean?"

"I'm not giving up." He bounced the ball twice and shot it into the hoop. Then he turned to her with a smile on his lips but determination in his eyes. "I'll see those legs eventually."

Chapter Five

"I'm leaving now," Ronnie said into the phone. She turned out the light in the back office.

"All right. See you in a little bit, nugget," her father said.

Ronnie set the alarm and extinguished the light in the lobby. Seconds later, she locked the front door and gave it a good shove to make sure the bolt caught. The night was a little chilly and she shivered, pulling the fleece jacket tighter around her shoulders.

At half past seven, it was quiet, with all the employees gone and inadequate lights casting shadows in the parking lot along the mostly quiet street. A lone car cruised by, slowing when it approached the red traffic light a hundred yards away, and accelerating when the light turned to green.

The shop closed at six, but Ronnie sometimes stayed behind an hour or two working on administrative tasks she preferred not to tackle during regular business hours. Paperwork was her least favorite part of working at the auto shop, but necessary. Her greatest joy, however, came from working on cars.

Because her father didn't trust just anyone to watch her, he'd started bringing her to the shop at an early age and made keeping an eye on her part of the duties of his office manager at the time. Her earliest memory was of being five years old and hanging out with the men in the garage and handing them tools, or watching from a safe position on a stool, admiring their work and inhaling the intoxicating smell of oil, grease, and sweat.

Twenty-one years later, she worked at the same spot, but the mechanics had come and gone over the years, Alfred staying around the longest.

Her father negotiated a ten-year lease before he turned over the reins to her, but the lease was coming to an end. Ronnie mulled the rent increase notice she received from the company managing the property. She worried she couldn't meet all of her obligations with such a decline in revenue over the past few months, and hesitated to sign the new lease.

She'd run ads in the paper to boost business and listed coupon codes on the bulletin boards of nearby stores and the local laundromat, but none of those efforts created the surge she'd hoped for.

Her mind was so distracted by business problems, she didn't notice the dark image coming toward her until he was only a few feet away. She pulled up short and stared at the stranger, fingers tightening around a chrome crescent wrench she carried low against her leg during the nights she worked late.

She immediately shifted into a fighting stance, feet spread wider than her hips, tension in her abdominal muscles. "What do you want?" she asked in a loud voice.

"Do you have a few bucks I can borrow to get something to eat?"

In the dim lights of the parking lot, she clearly saw the red dirt covering the man's tattered clothes. A foul smell came from him, and she barely restrained from plugging her nose with her fingertips. She'd seen him around a few times, walking along the roadway during the daytime. One time, she ran him off the property for begging customers for money.

"I have a few dollars for you," a male said, coming out of the shadows.

Ronnie's shoulders sagged at the sight of Diego. His broad body appeared even broader in a black jacket, and the dusky tint of his skin appeared darker in the night. The brim of a D&M Towing cap covered his dark hair and hid his green eyes under shadow.

The man's previously earnest and intense expression shifted into one of alarm, and Ronnie wondered if he had specifically been waiting for her. The thought made her very uneasy. This stretch of road was fairly busy during the day, but at night, much quieter with less traffic.

Diego pulled out a few dollars and extended his hand. The man hesitated, eyes darting between the couple. Then he grabbed the cash. "Th-thank you," he said in a hushed voice.

"You're welcome. But it's not a good idea for you to be hanging around here at night anymore," Diego said in a flinty voice, unsmiling.

"Won't do that again," the man mumbled, ducking his head. He stumbled away, once glancing over his shoulder as if worried Diego would suddenly grab him and snatch away the money.

When he'd disappeared into the night, Ronnie turned to Diego. "Thanks. I—"

"I told you about being here at night alone," Diego interrupted in a harsh voice.

Ronnie reared back. He had never spoken to her like that before. "Yes, I know you have."

"Why are you always here so late at night by yourself, anyway?"

"I have paperwork to do, and I prefer doing it at night, when it's quiet and there are no distractions," she said defensively.

"You need to cut that shit out." His eyebrows snapped together over his eyes.

Okay.

Granted, she needed to rethink her workday and avoid having to stay late when everyone else was gone. Even her father had warned her about leaving too late and insisted she call every night before she left so he could gauge how long it took for her to get home. He often pointed out that she was small in size, and from the time she was a child, he'd instilled in her the importance of being able to defend herself—and made sure she could.

"I have this." She held up the heavy tool. "No one can mess with me."

"If I sneaked up on you, I could grab you and you wouldn't have time to use that thing."

"Jeez, relax."

"It's not a joke, Veronica." Diego ran a hand along the back of his neck and rotated his shoulders.

Properly reprimanded, Ronnie fell quiet. Neither of them spoke. Another car rolled by, its noisy muffler disturbing the silence.

"The back lot looks nice," Ronnie said quietly.

"You beat me, so I made the guys clean up."

"Nice to know you keep your promises and pay your debts."

They fell quiet again. Then he said, "You'll be happy to know I spent the afternoon filing for title on the abandoned vehicles."

"*What?*" Ronnie said, exaggerating the surprise and skepticism in her voice.

He threw back his head in a full belly laugh. She preferred that expression on his face, much more than the anger from before.

"Smart ass."

Ronnie grinned, her pulse doing a weird racing thing. His presence charged her, the way jumper cables recharged a battery.

"I'll let you know which ones I want you to work on. Maybe I deserve a reward," he added slyly.

"You couldn't resist, could you?" she asked.

"I can't seem to help myself when I'm around you," he said in a subdued voice.

Her pulse quickened. "Is that right?" she said in a flippant tone, pretending not to care.

"Can't, even though you give me so much grief." He glanced at his black wristwatch. "Let's go get something to eat. My treat."

"No, thanks."

Diego leaned in, and she could clearly see his eyes. They searched her face. "What are you afraid of?"

Rejection.

"I'm not afraid," Ronnie lied, shoving her empty hand into the overalls' pockets. "I'm not that hungry. I'll probably grab a burger and eat it on the way home."

"Then let's go to dinner another night."

"No."

He laughed. "Do I smell or something? Is it my breath?"

"No, it's…"

"What?" he pushed.

She swallowed, unsure how to express the hesitation, even to herself. Sharing her thoughts meant laying bare her insecurities. "I'm not the kind of woman you date."

Men said they wanted a low-maintenance woman, and when they found out she was into sports, they became excited about someone sharing their interests. They loved the thought of not getting dragged to chick flicks or sitting around shopping malls holding packages and purses. Yet the unvarnished truth was that every characteristic men said they *didn't* want in a woman was a prevalent trait in the women they fell for. Never failed.

Ronnie should know. She'd played matchmaker to plenty of female acquaintances with her male friends over the years. They all had boyfriends. She didn't.

The one man she'd thought she had a connection with simply treated her as an interlude and moved on to a woman who fit into a more traditional gender role. Ronnie was good enough to hang out with but not good enough to date.

"You don't know the kind of women I date," Diego said.

"Trust me, I know."

"Oh really? What kind of women do you think I like?"

"Women like the blonde from Saturday, with the Volkswagen." His type always went for the delicate flowers who wore skirts and heels and needed help getting down from a truck. "I wouldn't be surprised if you're seeing her. She certainly left no doubt that she was interested." Her stomach contracted as she waited for a response.

"She's married," Diego said flatly.

"Oh, I'm sorry," Ronnie said, even though she was anything but. "Better luck next time."

Diego observed her silence, but his scrutiny quickly became unbearable.

"What?" Ronnie asked sharply.

"Did my answer change your mind about dinner?"

"No." Ronnie saw his flirtations for what they were. A game. Nothing more.

He gave a short laugh. "I'll see you tomorrow, Veronica."

"Why do you do that?" Ronnie asked.

His brow furrowed. "Do what?"

"Call me Veronica." Whenever he said her name, a fluttery sensation invaded her stomach.

"That's your name, isn't it?"

"It is, but no one calls me Veronica. Everybody calls me Ronnie." Everybody but him.

"I like Veronica better."

"So you go around renaming people with names you like better?" Ronnie asked, itching for a fight but not knowing why.

"Veronica is your real name," Diego pointed out, his voice slow and even, like a teacher explaining complicated calculus to a five-year-old. "I didn't rename you. Everyone else did. And Ronnie sounds like a man's name. But if you don't want me to call—"

"No, it's…" The thought of him stopping sent her

into an unforeseen panic. Her stomach trembled, and she shrugged dismissively, but she definitely didn't want him to stop. "It's fine. I just wondered, that's all."

"*Bueno*." Diego stifled a yawn. "I'm tired and hungry. Maybe you don't care much about dinner, but I have a taste for steak tonight, so I can't stay here all night watching out for you. Get in your truck." He started away from her.

"I never asked you to watch out for me." Ronnie huffed. She could take care of herself. She marched toward her blue Nissan.

Settling into the vehicle, she tossed the wrench on the floor and stuck the key in the ignition. Once again she heard the words he'd said.

I can't stay here all night watching out for you.

She sat in the dark cab but didn't drive away, and neither did Diego. He sat in his personal vehicle, a black behemoth with a hemi engine and the ability to tow thirty-one thousand pounds. A beast of a machine. Sturdy and strong, like its owner.

She watched the minutes on the face of her phone advance slowly, one after the other. She waited a full five minutes, but he never moved.

Finally, she started the engine and drove out of the lot. He followed behind her and went in the opposite direction.

Diego worked late every night she did and left around the same time. Always. Once or twice might be coincidence, but every time indicated a pattern.

Ronnie eased to a traffic light and stopped on red. She acknowledged what she'd never noticed before, and what she was certain Diego would never admit. He wasn't staying late because he had work to do. He stayed behind because of her.

She smiled through the biting of her lip.

Though she was perfectly capable of taking care of herself, her insides warmed at the thought of Diego sticking around to make sure she was safe.

To keep an eye on her. To watch out for her.

Chapter Six

Stressed from almost being picked off the highway when a speeding motorist sideswiped his truck after he and his entire team went to the scene of a multi-car accident, Diego welcomed the relaxing chaos and noise of Dilligan's Sports Pub. This wasn't his usual hangout, but the bar he and his cousin used to frequent was shut down for health code violations.

Damn shame, too. He missed their spicy wings.

"Oops, excuse me." A waitress with curly black hair bounced against him and sloshed beer on his arm.

"That's okay," Diego said. The place was crowded, but that made the second time she bumped into him during a fifteen-minute period. She was either the clumsiest waitress he'd ever met, or she was making a pass at him.

She swiped the spilled beer off his wrist with her thumb and sucked the finger into her mouth. Tossing him a come-hither look, she strutted away with an extra switch in her walk.

Okay, then. Mystery solved. The next time she passed his way, he was getting her number.

Monitors on the tables and giant TVs on the walls displayed sporting events taking place around the country, but tonight the main attraction was the NBA playoffs. The six-four shooting guard for the Miami Heat shot a three-pointer in a battle for the Eastern Conference semifinals title against the Atlanta Hawks. The play cut the lead to five points.

Diego pumped his fist in a loud cheer. His cousin, Tomas, cursed in Spanish beside him. Tomas was taller than Diego, with his brown hair pulled back into a ponytail by a leather strap.

"I can't believe it," Tomas muttered, whiskey-colored eyes flashing in annoyed disappointment. He shook his head in disgust. "Goddammit, they had a twenty-one point lead in the first half."

Diego laughed and took a sip of Coke. "We're going to stomp all over the Hawks on our way to another championship."

Ryan, Tomas's best friend, looked past Tomas to Diego. Dark-haired and blue-eyed, he had garnered the attention of two women sitting in a booth across the room. They'd sent a waitress over to invite him to their table for a drink, but he shot them down from a distance when he flashed his wedding band.

"You live in Atlanta now. You should be cheering for the Hawks," Ryan said.

"He has no loyalty," Tomas muttered.

"This isn't about loyalty. It's about championships, and once we take the lead, it's over." He swiped a hand across his throat like a knife. "The Hawks can't take the heat."

The game broke for commercial and Tomas turned his back on the television. Leaning across the antique bar's gleaming surface, he asked, "What's the latest with D&M Towing?"

"Good so far. Business is steady, and I hired someone to work on a proposal to handle the towing for a shopping plaza five miles from the company. Hell, I'm even getting along with my neighbor now."

"The mechanic?" Tomas asked, a smile of amusement crossing his features. He thought it was funny Diego couldn't get past Ronnie's icy exterior, no matter how hard he tried.

"She's been a lot sweeter lately." In all honesty, he loved messing with her and purposely provoked her. When she came at him, hands on her hips, brown eyes flashing, she made his nuts ache. All he could think about was fucking all that hostility out of her.

One time. All he needed was one time with Ronnie Taylor, and he'd have her purring like a kitten instead of scratching like a lioness.

"Hey, fellas, can I get you anything else?" The perky bartender with cocoa skin and a tousled pixie flashed a smile at the three of them, but her gaze settled on Diego, the only unmarried one of the trio.

"I'm good," he said.

She didn't wait for a response from the other two, and walked away.

Tomas elbowed him. "She's obviously interested. What's the matter with you?"

What was the matter with him? She was definitely stacked. His eyes dropped to the way the snug jeans fit over her big, beautiful ass.

"Guess I'm not in the mood." Lately, a pervasive restlessness plagued him. More and more he bypassed the easy lay, causing his mind to be unsettled. He set his glass on the bar top. "I need to take a leak."

He took off toward the bathrooms and worked his way to the back of the bar, passing two other rooms filled with occupants. A roar went up from the group inside one of them. He glanced in and saw a bunch of men crowded around a pool table. Must be a great game.

Minutes later, Diego exited the restroom and heard loud cheers from the same room. Once again, he peered in, but this time an unexpected sight snagged his attention. Ronnie held a pool stick in the middle of the men, entrenched in what looked to be an intense game of pool. Brow furrowed, she circled the rectangle with slow strides, sizing up the next shot.

She stopped with her back to him, so engrossed in the game she never saw him standing outside the door.

"Eight ball, corner pocket."

The giant gray shirt she wore looked three sizes too big, so long the hem landed at the middle of her thighs, and so wide the fabric swallowed her body. Skinny jeans and a pair of tennis shoes completed the casual outfit. Nothing about her screamed sex appeal, but Diego's stomach clenched as he watched her bend over the table, butt sticking out, to line up the shot.

The balls cracked against each other and the eight ball flew into the hole in the corner.

Howls of joy filled the room, and men started smacking Ronnie on the back and shoulders. An urge to shield her from the enthusiastic blows tightened Diego's muscles and he launched into the room. Catching himself, he pulled up short, frowning at the rough way they handled her. But Ronnie was clearly tougher than she looked. She took each blow without a hint of discomfort.

All the men laughed right along with her except her opponent—a black male standing across the table from her and wearing a surly expression after being spanked, four of his balls still left on the table.

Greenbacks started changing hands. They'd obviously placed bets on the game. Ronnie herself received a thick-looking wad she stuffed into the front pocket of her jeans.

"Who's next?" she asked, resting the pool stick on its end like a staff.

"Not me. I'm out," one guy said, throwing up his hands.

"No one's brave enough to play me?" Her eyes swept the room from left to right.

Each man shook his head.

Goddamn. Diego curled his lip in disgust. Ronnie intimidated a bunch of so-called men twice her size.

A heavy-set brown-skinned male, wearing a tight-fitting Atlanta Hawks T-shirt and his worn leather belt battling the bulge around his waist, stood at least a foot over Ronnie. He pointed down at her head. "Anybody else want to challenge my girl?"

"Come on, you guys," she needled the men. "Nobody?"

The man acting like a promoter held up a wad of cash. "There's money to be made if you can beat her."

"Ain't nobody stupid enough to play Ronnie or bet against her," one man piped up.

"There're a few dummies," someone else said.

The men laughed. Three of them grimaced,

suggesting they must have been the dummies who bet against her.

"Nobody's brave enough to challenge my girl?"

The men averted their eyes and an awkward silence descended on the room, disrupted only by the play-by-play from the announcers analyzing the NBA game projected on the only television in the room.

"I'll play her," Diego said.

All eyes turned to him, and Ronnie swung around. Her eyes widened in surprise and he sauntered closer. She watched him warily, and he eyed her right back.

"You don't want to do that, bro," someone said. "She beats the pants off of every man she plays."

"She's never played me." Diego hooked a thumb in his belt loop.

"Put your money where your mouth is," said the one acting like her promoter.

"How much are we talking?" Diego asked.

"An even hundred if you want to play."

"You're about to be out one hundred dollars, buddy," someone near the back cracked.

There were a series of soft chuckles.

Diego fished out his wallet and removed five crisp bills. He slapped them onto the green felt and fixed his gaze on Ronnie. "We'll see about that."

Chapter Seven

Ronnie folded her arms and flicked a dismissive gaze over Diego. Clearly, she didn't think him much of an opponent.

"I'm the reigning champ," she said, sticking her nose in the air.

Her promoter flung an arm around her, and Diego smothered the urge to knock the man's meaty arm off her slender shoulders.

"She's only been beaten once, bro, and that night she had the flu."

Diego ignored him, keeping his gaze constant and on Ronnie. "I put up my money—now put up yours."

Her mouth turned into a round pucker of deep thought. With difficulty, Diego dragged his eyes from the enticing fullness of those lips.

Ronnie counted one hundred dollars and dropped it onto the stack of twenties. The promoter swiped up the cash. "Once again, it's on!" he crowed.

"I need to make one change to the bet," Diego

said.

Ronnie raised a brow. "What kind of change?"

"If I win, I won't take your money."

"Ha!" the promoter interjected. "You were never going to get it."

Diego ignored him and zeroed in on Ronnie's lips. Full on the bottom and the top. He really wanted to know what they tasted like. How they felt. "If I win…" He let the sentence trail off dramatically before delivering his ultimatum: "…you give me a kiss."

Murmurs filled the room, and Ronnie's face settled into lines of alarm. "No way."

"You picked the wrong one, pal. Ronnie doesn't swing that way," one of the men said.

A few awkward chuckles sprinkled throughout the room.

Ronnie swung her head in the direction of the joker. "Shut up. Just because I won't sleep with you doesn't mean I'm gay," she snapped. The men settled down and she switched her attention to Diego. "No."

"Why not?" Diego asked. She was so adamantly against the idea that he became more determined to get her to agree.

"No. That's final. Let's go back to the money. You win, I give you one hundred dollars. I win, you give me one hundred dollars. You can make other bets on the spread."

"I don't want your money," Diego said.

"That's all that's on offer."

"A kiss," he pushed back.

Her lips flattened, and he imagined kissing them again. He wasn't giving up.

A solid-looking male, a few inches taller than

Diego, came up behind Ronnie and dropped a heavy hand on her shoulder. "You're not going to lose, Ronnie. Go ahead. I put my money on you."

Diego waited for her response.

"I'm not giving you a kiss." Ronnie glanced at his lips and then quickly found his eyes again, biting the corner of her mouth.

Diego smiled. The little firecracker seemed to be having the same thoughts he did. Maybe she wasn't as immune as she pretended to be. "Then all you have to do is beat me," he said.

"Come on, Ronnie, you can take him." Her hype man squeezed her shoulder.

Diego held her gaze. She wouldn't look away, and neither would he.

Tense seconds ticked by while everyone waited. A roar went up from the crowd in the stadium at the NBA final, but Diego didn't let the game distract him.

Ronnie took a deep breath. "Fine," she said, lips so tight they barely moved.

"Yes!" Her promoter turned back to the room. "Place your bets, place your bets. Who's got Ronnie and who's got—Hey, what's your name?"

"Diego."

Ronnie eyed him with suspicion. "I'm not going easy on you," she warned in a fierce whisper.

Diego angled closer. "I wouldn't expect anything less," he whispered back.

They held each other's gazes for a little bit longer as the men around them moved into a flurry of action and her hype man collected the funds, noting who bet on whom, the spread, etc.

At long last, Ronnie wheeled away and marched over to the other side of the pool table. While

Ronnie's promoter racked the balls, Diego checked out the sticks on the wall. One after the other, he bounced each across his palm, gauging the weight until he found a suitable one. It wasn't the same as the one he had at home, but it would suffice.

Diego waved his hand at the table. "Ladies first."

Without a word, Ronnie removed the triangle and bent over the table, lined up the tip of her stick, and with a firm stroke slammed the cue ball into the other balls and scattered them into all corners. Red flew into a hole.

"Solids," Ronnie said.

Eyes narrowed, she sized up the next play. Diego fixated on the tight line of her body bent over the table. Toned arms, pert bottom sticking out. His breathing became shallow, his loins heavy with the idea of stepping behind her, and cupping and lifting her hips against his groin.

Calling the next shot, Ronnie tapped the blue solid into the side pocket. She missed the next one and stepped back so Diego could take over.

He swiped chalk onto the tip of the stick and rotated his shoulders, scanning the layout before him. He analyzed the position of the balls and mentally drew lines across the table. Satisfied with his decision, he called a shot and knocked the striped ball into the corner pocket. As the group watched him hit balls into the holes two more times, tension radiated in the air.

Ronnie took control of the table again, and three shots later, it was Diego's turn once more. She'd warmed up during the first match up and was better than he expected. He couldn't prolong the game anymore or risked losing.

The next shot would be a kick shot, where he bounced the cue ball off the rail cushion and knocked the striped ball into the corner. He called the move and the group around him shook their heads in disbelief, some of them chuckling softly at the unlikelihood of success.

Ronnie didn't laugh, though. She watched him closely, perhaps recognizing he was better than he'd originally let on.

Which he was.

Diego rubbed chalk on the tip of the pool stick. "Did I mention I made it to the World Pool Masters Tournament?" Bending over the table, he lined up the shot. He was a master of trick shots. "They called me *el Brujo*. The Magician." His eyes glided up to Ronnie's. A hard swallow moved along the length of her slender throat, and his mouth lifted into a slow smile of victory.

He hit the cue ball and it bounced off the side and flew down in triangle formation to knock the orange stripe into the corner pocket.

Someone behind him cursed and the tension in the room thickened. There was a lot of money at stake.

"Yellow, corner pocket, and then green in the side pocket."

"Hell no," Ronnie's hype man said.

"Want to put money on it?" Diego asked.

The guy shut up real quick and fell back.

Diego sat on the edge of the table and held the pool stick almost perpendicular. This was a tricky shot better done with his own stick, but he was confident he could do it.

The white ball knocked in the yellow, and spinning rapidly, circled around to the green and tapped it in.

The room erupted.

"Whoa!"

"Holy shit!"

Diego shot a look at Ronnie. She silently observed him, confidence swept from her face. He cleaned off the table and called the last shot. "Eight ball, side pocket." He hit the cue ball low and hard. The eight ball sank into the hole and the white one rolled back toward him.

Noise erupted in the room, a mixture of cheers of disbelief that someone had finally beaten Ronnie, but also low groans at the money they'd lost.

He and Ronnie stared across the table at each other. Her features appeared decidedly grim, all emotion wiped away.

"You tricked me," she said.

Diego almost felt bad for her. Almost. But not quite.

He grinned. "Somebody owes me a kiss."

Chapter Eight

Ronnie's heart trembled against her ribs and clammy hands held tight to the stick in her hands. Diego didn't just beat her—he whooped her ass. She couldn't ever remember being whooped so soundly by anyone before, and with such style. That last trick shot had been a thing of beauty. She admired him while simultaneously she was disappointed in herself for the loss.

"I'll gladly give you the money," she offered, a last-ditch effort to renege on the wager she'd never wanted in the first place.

"Told you I don't want your money," he said.

She bit her lip and resigned to her fate.

A kiss. From Diego. A man who annoyed the living daylights out of her.

A man she wanted.

A man who flaunted his sex appeal and was absolutely not her type. Ugh. If he wasn't her type, why did her heart flutter so fast, like a flower petal tossed in hurricane winds? Why did she remain glued to the spot, excited but terrified, feet practically bolted to the floor?

All around her, money changed hands. The few who'd wagered against her collected a considerable sum.

One guy patted Diego on the shoulder. "Thanks, pal. Never thought I'd see the day Ronnie got her ass whooped."

She glared at the turncoat before shifting her gaze to Diego. "Let's get this over with. But not here."

His eyebrows rose. "You want to go somewhere private?" The question sounded like an intimate invitation.

"Somewhere less crowded," Ronnie corrected. If she had to kiss him, she'd do so without a bunch of onlookers watching their every move.

He gestured at the door. "Lead the way."

He was gloating. Smug. Loving every minute of his victory and her loss.

Ronnie marched ahead out the door, turning down the hallway near the bathrooms. She swung left at the backdoor exit, an area quieter than the loud, raucous poolroom.

Balling her fists, she took a deep breath and swung around to face Diego. He stepped closer, and her skin heated. Considerably taller than her, he seemed to take up much of the space in the hall.

She flexed her fingers in preparation.

His eyes narrowed on her. "Is it true what that guy said back there?"

"Is what true?" she asked.

"You don't like men?" He actually seemed concerned.

"You won. What difference does it make?"

"It makes a difference. I don't want to make you uncomfortable."

Uncomfortable either way, she knew what he meant. He'd offered a way out, and for a few seconds she wavered, tempted to seize the opportunity and escape from this predicament.

But she didn't. She lowered her gaze to his mouth, and then wished she hadn't. He had a fleshy bottom lip and a curved upper lip. Truth be told, she was curious. What would his kiss be like? Firm or soft? Dry or wet? Was he a good kisser or a bad one?

Looking the way he did, she couldn't imagine he was bad, but it was possible. That didn't stop her heart from racing, though. Nor her stomach from tightening in anticipation.

"It's not true," Ronnie answered, her voice unnaturally hoarse. "I like men."

Her cheeks burned. Admitting her preference out loud sounded weird, but over the years, she'd overheard all types of comments and should be used to them by now. People guessed all sorts of reasons why she couldn't get and keep a man.

"If she'd just be a little more feminine."

"She's just so boyish."

"Poor thing. She's too short and too skinny. Men like real women with curves."

"She knows a lot of men. Why can't she get one?"

"Let's get this over with," Ronnie said. Back rigid, she closed her eyes, puckered her lips, and waited.

Nothing happened.

She peered through the slits in her eyes at Diego, who simply stared at her.

"What are you doing?" he asked.

"Getting ready for the kiss," Ronnie explained.

He licked his lips, and she watched the way his tongue slid across his full bottom lip, moistening the thick flesh. She inhaled deeply and ran a hand along the outside of her shirt-covered hips.

"Are we going to do this or not?" She'd expected to sound a lot meaner, but a faint tremor had crept into her voice, and she hoped he didn't notice.

He considered her with narrowed eyes and cupped her jaw with one hand, the calloused thumb of the other hand moved along the length of her throat. Sparks flew across her skin.

"We're going to do this," he confirmed. His voice had lowered a bit to a sexier tone—one that washed over her with unexpected sensuality. "But not tonight."

"Wh-what?" Ronnie said, voice awash in dismay.

"I'll kiss you when I'm ready." Diego dropped his hands and took a couple steps back.

"You will kiss me now!" The words flew past her lips before she could stop them. Ronnie inhaled sharply, mortified at the angry demand.

The right corner of his mouth ticked up and amusement filled his eyes. "Now, now, I won the bet. I get to decide when I collect."

"How long do you plan—"

Diego pressed a finger to her lips. Resting a hand above her head, he leaned in and Ronnie backed into the wall. "I'm in charge, and I don't have to tell you anything. I'll let you know when I'm ready for my kiss." He blew an air kiss, and the quick smacking sound triggered the tightening of her nipples.

He was only doing this to annoy her, but now he held the power, able to approach her at any time and demand a kiss at will. Ronnie balled her hands into angry fists.

"See you tomorrow, *mami*." Diego strutted off and left Ronnie behind to fume alone.

****

"What happened to you?" Tomas asked when Diego walked up.

"Saw someone I knew."

"We thought we were going to have to send a search party after you," Ryan joked.

"No need for all that." Diego shoved aside his watery Coke and signaled for the bartender. "Another one of these, please."

"Coming right up," the bartender said.

"Are you okay, *primo*?" Tomas asked.

"I'm fine." Diego grinned to allay his cousin's concerns.

When the drink arrived, he took a few swallows and focused on the NBA game, but the men running back and forth down the court held little interest for him. Even when his beloved Miami Heat expanded the lead to eleven points, he couldn't conjure his earlier enthusiasm.

All he could think about was how he turned the tables on Ronnie. Recalling the fierce look in her eyes and the demand to kiss her *now*—oh damn, how he'd wanted to slam her against the wall and devour her mouth—he laughed softly to himself.

Diego sipped his soda.

He had her right where he wanted her.

****

Ronnie pressed her hands to her head. What was happening? An hour ago she was playing pool and not thinking about Diego's lips anywhere near her.

Now, the thought of his mouth consumed her. Denying her only made her want the kiss more.

She went into the ladies' bathroom and, bracing her hands on the sink, stared at her reflection.

She didn't want this queasiness in her stomach. The tightness in her breasts. The longing for more. The last time she felt anything close to these sensations had been with Leonard.

A slice of pain twisted in her chest, and she closed her eyes.

Sighing, she opened them again and saw anxiety reflected back at her.

Friends since high school, she and Leonard did everything together—attend sporting events, play basketball, and he often spent time at her house on Sundays when her father fired up the grill. Friends to lovers. What could be better? It never occurred to her he would break her heart, but that was exactly what he did.

He snuck around behind her back with a woman the complete opposite of Ronnie. Even her name, Dahlia, conjured images of flowers and sugar and spice and all things nice.

Ronnie saw them one evening while out to dinner with her cousin, Anika. Dahlia wore her long hair down and a figure-hugging dress, while Leonard looked downright dashing in a suit and tie.

Unnoticed, she watched Leonard help Dahlia into her chair. When he sat down, they held hands across the table. The sight of him gazing so tenderly into another woman's eyes filled her with jealous rage.

He never helped her into her chair. He never held her hand or looked at her like that.

She made a horrible scene in the restaurant, and

Anika forcibly dragged her out. Later, in addition to being mortified by her behavior, she'd felt like such an idiot thinking about all the times she worked on his car and his family members' cars for free, and how he'd insisted she wasn't "like other girls." Back then she thought the words were a compliment, but came to learn they were anything but.

Ronnie splashed water on her face and straightened her shoulders. She couldn't stay in the bathroom forever.

She left and went to the front of Dilligan's, catching sight of Diego at the bar, in conversation with two other men. She made a beeline for the door and, once outside, trotted to her Nissan 4 X 4.

Gunning the engine, she squealed out of the parking lot.

Desperate to escape Diego Molina and everything he made her feel.

Chapter Nine

On Saturday, Ronnie left work early and went to Deluxe Barber Lounge to get a line up. When she pushed open the door, the barbers and regulars called out a greeting.

"Hey, Ronnie!"

She waved hello and plunked down in one of the chairs along the wall to wait for Jacob to finish a teenager's haircut. She scanned the magazines on the table. Passing over a tattered, well-handled copy of *King* with the picture of a scantily clad Melyssa Ford on the cover, she picked up the latest issue of *Sports Illustrated*.

Sometimes Ronnie stopped in even if she didn't need a cut, to shoot the breeze with the men and listen to the old heads talk about how they'd "seen some things," as they liked to say. The best stories came from first-hand accounts of major events she'd read about in the history books. Civil Rights marches. The Vietnam War. Fascinating stories emerged each time she visited.

The all-male atmosphere included men of all ages. From Tarik, the eight-year-old who came regularly with his father, to Buck, a relic from the Civil Rights movement who'd participated in demonstrations with the likes of Ambassador Andrew Young and Congressman John Lewis.

Ronnie had been coming here since her teens, when she cut off her hair and adopted a maintenance-free hairstyle. At first the men were careful around her, refraining from cursing and using code words to discuss sexual topics or avoiding them altogether. After joining a heated argument and quoting sports stats that even some of the men didn't know, she'd impressed them. Nowadays, they didn't see her as the typical woman. She was one of the guys, and as such, was treated with the same indifference as any man who walked through the door.

"What'll it be today?" Jacob asked when she sat in the chair. He was older than Ronnie, somewhere in his late forties. Good-looking with a full beard that showed a little bit of gray and gave him a distinguished appearance.

"The usual. Neat and tight, please," she said.

"What's the latest with your pop?"

"He's doing fine. Eating right, like he's supposed to, which is not easy to get him to do."

Jacob chuckled. "When you get to a certain age, like your pop, a man ought to be able to eat what he wants." He snapped the black cape around her neck. "I could create a nice design for you," he offered hopefully. He'd been trying to put a design in her hair to show off his skills for the longest time.

"I'll leave that for the younger set," she said,

smiling at him in the mirror.

"You ain't too far from the younger set yourself," Jacob pointed out, picking up the scissors.

Ronnie relaxed in the chair and, after joking with him and the other men, mentioned having to take off from work to drive her father to and from cataract surgery.

"I'm worried," she admitted. The doctor had assured her and Ezekiel they had nothing to worry about, but Ronnie still harbored some fear.

"Don't worry," Jacob said. "It's routine surgery."

Several of the men spoke up and reassured her. They pointed out that either they or their parents had gone through the same surgery with no problems.

"I'm glad to hear it." Their answers put her mind at ease.

"Poppa Ezekiel still beating off the old ladies at church?" an attractive, twenty-something barber across the room asked.

"Yes, and that will never change," Ronnie answered. "As far as my father's concerned, no one holds a candle to my mother."

Jacob gently twisted her head so he could taper the hair at her left temple. "Rosie was something else, but that's a long time to go without a woman." The clippers buzzed softly as he worked.

"You knew my mother?" Ronnie asked. She didn't talk about her mother much since she'd been dead for a long time, so it took her by surprise that Jacob knew her.

"Not well. Met her a couple of times, long before your time, from back in the neighborhood. I remember when she and your daddy started dating. Hey, Buck, you remember when Rosie and Ezekiel

One of the Guys

were dating back in the day?"

He called out to a man seated on one of the chairs, wearing an Irish flat cap and glasses. Buck looked over large, black-framed spectacles from the newspaper. He was an old head, always dressed sharp in a button-down shirt and a sweater vest from what must be a larger collection. Winter, spring, summer, or fall, Buck wore the same uniform, only different colors.

"Sure do. Best girl in the neighborhood. Rosie was sweet as could be, fine as wine, and way too good for him, with his old ass."

The men around him chuckled and Ronnie smiled. "Hey, you're talking about my daddy. With *your* old ass."

"Just telling the truth." Buck snapped the newspaper and went back to reading.

"Everybody was jealous of Ezekiel for landing someone that fine couldn't nobody else get. Her parents brought her up real strict."

Ronnie's grandparents, long dead, had been devout Christians, and their protectiveness over her mother came as no surprise. At thirty-six, her father had been fifteen years her mother's senior. He told her once about how he'd pursued her, carefully at first, proving himself to her parents with his work ethic and polite manners. He'd sealed the deal with them by regularly attending church services.

"Rosie was sweet as could be, but she wasn't no pushover, and pretty and prim and proper." Jacob twisted Ronnie's head to work on the right side. "Damn shame she died so young."

Pain pricked the middle of Ronnie's chest. She wished she could remember something, anything,

63

about her mother. A heavy knot from missing mother/daughter bonding reared its ugly head in her stomach. Her father did a great job on his own, and whenever moments of uncertainty arose—such as around the time she started menstruating—the women in the family helped him. But Ronnie knew there was nothing like having a mother in her life.

"I firmly believe your daddy will find somebody else one of these days," Jacob said.

"You think so?" Ronnie looked at him in the mirror.

"Absolutely. One day you'll be gone, and he'll be by himself, and the Good Book says it's not good for man to be alone. Thing is, your daddy's old school. Gotta let him pursue. Not pursue him. That's why those women at church don't stand a chance. Besides, mean and ornery as he is, he's got to find someone to change his disposition, or he'll never make it past the Pearly Gates."

Ronnie thought about her father and Miss Loretta, wondering if their neighbor could be what her father needed to change his disposition.

Smiling to herself, she got an idea of how to get them to spend time together.

****

When Ronnie arrived at home, she saw Miss Loretta bent over the open hood of her car.

She walked across the lawn to her neighbor's side. "What's the problem?" she asked.

"I'm not sure. When I try to start the car, it makes a strange sound and won't start." A frown wrinkled Miss Loretta's brow. "Don't ask me why I have the hood up. I don't know what I'm looking for." She laughed, placing a hand on her chest and looking a little embarrassed.

Ronnie smiled. "Crank it and I'll see if I can figure out the problem."

Miss Loretta went to the driver's side of the vehicle and sat in the car. She turned the key in the ignition and the engine coughed, and then died on a clicking sound. Probably a dead battery. Ronnie could use her battery tester but a better idea came to mind.

"I may have to let my dad listen to this. I'm not sure what the problem is."

Miss Loretta's eyes lit up. "Oh. Do you think Ezekiel would mind?" She patted her gray and black wig.

"Not at all. He's a better mechanic than I am, so I'm sure he can figure it out."

"Wonderful."

"I'll go get him." Ronnie turned away and then snapped her fingers as if she suddenly remembered something. "Could I ask a huge favor of you?"

"Certainly. What is it, dear?"

"In a couple of weeks, Daddy's going to have cataract surgery, and he needs someone to take him to the surgery center in the morning and pick him up a few hours later when they're done. Do you mind?"

"I would love...I mean, I don't mind at all."

"You're sure?"

"Yes, yes."

"Great. Thank you so much. Give me a few minutes."

Ronnie left her neighbor's yard, barely able to contain her excitement. Her father was descending the stairs when she entered the house.

"I saw you next door. What did Loretta want?" he asked.

"Her car won't start. Could you look at it for her?"

"I'm not her personal mechanic."

"No, but you could do a good deed, considering you don't have any problems eating all the baked goods she brings by."

"It would be rude to refuse."

Ronnie's eyebrow jerked upward.

"I don't ask for them," Ezekiel said defensively. He stood on the bottom stair.

"And she didn't ask for your help. I offered on your behalf." Ronnie passed him on the way up.

"All right," he grumbled.

"Take the battery tester," Ronnie said, continuing to climb.

"If you know what's wrong, why do I need to go over there?" he called after her.

"I don't know for sure what's wrong. That's why you're taking the tester." Ronnie paused on the staircase. "And by the way, she'll be taking you to your surgery appointment."

"Why can't you? What's going on?"

Ronnie didn't answer and ran up the stairs, grinning to herself.

Chapter Ten

For the second time that morning, Diego asked to speak to Ronnie, but Alfred insisted she was too busy to come to the front.

The first few days after the night at Dilligan's, each time he approached Ronnie she either stiffened, a wary expression in her brown eyes, or looked ready to jump out of her skin. She fidgeted with her keys or watched him from the corner of her eye when he showed her a couple of cars he recently got the title on. Starting Wednesday, however, she'd steered clear of him altogether. She did an excellent job of avoiding him, and Diego's patience had worn thinner than tissue paper.

He scrutinized the activity in the garage through the glass that separated the waiting area from the mechanics' workspace. Although Ronnie and another technician worked on two vehicles, there was no conceivable reason why she couldn't take a few minutes to speak to him. Only two customers sat in the waiting area. A man wearing a suit and tie typed on a laptop. A woman sipped the free coffee Taylor Automotive provided and watched a rerun of *Family Feud* on the wall-mounted television.

"Did you tell her I came by earlier?" Diego asked.

"Yes, I did. Like I told you two hours ago, she's busy." Alfred gave him a blank stare.

Diego fisted his hands on the counter.

The owner of an '85 Corolla had never picked up the car after Diego towed it from the side of the road. The car was in good physical condition, and after cleaning it inside out, it sparkled.

Unfortunately, right when he was about to offer it for sale, the engine stopped turning over on a cold start, so he asked Ronnie to take a look at it. If she could fix the problem, he stood to make a couple thousand dollars. All he wanted was an update.

Ronnie glanced through the separating glass at him, and their eyes met and held. Heat rushed his chest and blood.

She broke eye contact first, donning a pair of protective goggles and going to work under a black SUV hoisted high on a lift.

Diego clenched his jaw. "It's really important—"

"I'll let her know you came by." Folding his arms, Alfred stood very still, a protective air about him.

Diego could only imagine what Ronnie had told the old man. He blew out a puff of frustrated air. "Thanks."

Before he left, his eyes were dragged once again to Ronnie. She couldn't avoid him forever.

****

"Knock, knock."

Ronnie twisted from the file cabinet and smiled

when she saw Alfred. "You heading out?"

He nodded. "Everything's locked up tight, except..." He glanced over his shoulder. Lowering his voice, he added, "Diego's sitting in the waiting room."

Crap. She should have left earlier.

"You need me to stick around?" Alfred asked.

"No, that's okay. Let him know I'll be right out."

"Will do."

Ronnie took her time filing the paperwork. He could wait, just like he was making her wait for that damn kiss. When she finished, she slammed the cabinet closed and, squaring her shoulders, marched into the waiting area.

"You wanted to see me?"

Diego rose from the chair, his jaw tight and green eyes boring into hers. He really knew how to make the tan work shirt and jeans look good. "You have time for me now?"

She glanced at the clock on the wall. "Not a whole lot of time, but I can fit you in."

"I'm so honored you could take time out of your busy schedule for me," he said sarcastically.

"You're so welcome." Ronnie smiled tightly. "How can I help you?"

Glowering at her, he didn't answer right away.

Avoiding him was a defense mechanism. At first her emotions vacillated between anxiety and disappointment that he didn't make a move. She was almost certain he purposely tortured her, standing too close when he pointed out the cars he wanted her to examine. Saying her name—Veronica—in a low, sexy voice that should be reserved for the bedroom.

She walked around like a skittish doe, anxious

about when a predator would charge out of the brush and claim its prize. To preserve her sanity, she avoided him altogether.

"I'm here about the Corolla," Diego said.

"I finished working on it this afternoon." She went over to the wall and started flipping switches. Bright overhead lights illuminated the garage.

"You could have told me you finished."

"I was going to tell you tomorrow." Or rather, have Alfred tell him.

"Were you?" Diego asked, skepticism coloring his voice.

"Of course," Ronnie answered in a breezy tone. She glanced over her shoulder and caught his eyes focused below her waist. Her hand stalled on the wall and her breath hitched.

Diego walked toward her, those intense sage-green eyes now focused on her mouth. She bit the inside of her bottom lip to keep it from quivering.

"Lead the way," he said.

Fumbling for the handle, Ronnie opened the door and led Diego to the far end of the garage. The Corolla sat in the last station. The previous owner had given it a new paint job. Instead of the factory tan, the car was silver and glowed like a bullet after Diego had it detailed and waxed.

Clearing her throat, she popped the hood and propped it open. "The problem stemmed from the carburetor. I cleaned the choke mechanism and replaced the linkage. She starts fine now."

Diego sank into the driver's seat and turned the key. The car immediately started. He hit the accelerator and revved the engine.

Grinning, he stepped out and patted the roof of

the car. "Perfect. How much do I owe you?"

She and Diego had agreed that if a repair fell below a certain dollar amount, she had permission to fix the vehicle without asking. Fixing the carburetor fell below the threshold.

Ronnie told him the total and he nodded.

"Not bad." Eyes on the parts under the hood, he came to stand beside her and she smelled him—that musky male scent of having worked all day, an intoxicating aroma that teased her nostrils and sent her pulse pounding.

She eased back one foot.

One of his eyebrows lifted toward the ceiling. "What's the matter with you?"

"You know what's the matter with me."

"No, I don't. Why don't you tell me."

Ronnie slammed down the hood. "You think this is a joke, don't you?"

His trademark sexy smile, where one side of his mouth lifted at the corner, made an appearance, infuriating her further.

"Why don't you go ahead and kiss me already?" she demanded.

The smile broadened to both sides of his face. "Anxious, are we?"

"I just don't want this damn kiss hanging over my head anymore."

"It's only been a week and one day."

"Eight days too long."

"Too bad. I'll kiss you when I'm ready and not a minute before." With a smug smile he moved past her.

"If you keep delaying I won't honor the bet."

"Yeah you will." He kept walking, unconcerned.

Uninterested. Not the least bit worried by the threat.

"Probably not that good anyway."

Diego froze. Turning slowly, eyes narrowed, he asked, "What did you say?"

Ronnie placed one hand on her hip and rolled her neck. "You heard me."

His nostrils flared and he stalked back to her. "Are you saying you think I can't kiss?"

Ronnie shrugged in a casual manner. "I'm saying I find it odd such a confident man won't kiss me. I have to assume there's a reason, and it's not because you don't want to. You've been after me for over a year. The only conclusion left is that you're afraid you won't measure up."

Fire sparked in his green eyes. "I'm an excellent kisser."

Ronnie flicked a dismissive look over him. "You have a nice body, but it's probably all window dressing."

She didn't believe those words for a minute. Diego didn't only look like the type to kiss well, he looked the type to curl toes and throw out backs. Big arms, big hands, powerful thighs. He had to be good in bed. It would be a travesty if he wasn't.

"I know you're purposely goading me, but you know what, I don't care. You want a kiss? I'll give you a kiss so good you'll forget your own name."

He advanced on her, intent in his eyes.

Ronnie's heart thumped against her ribs. She backed up, all bravado vanishing.

"When I get through with you, you won't remember the difference between a timing belt and a drive belt. When I get through with you, Veronica Taylor, you'll be begging for more than a kiss."

His hand whipped out, and warm, calloused fingers closed around the back of her neck. Diego dragged her into his embrace, and she slammed into his hard chest. The first press of his lips sent an explosive shock charging through her body. Her brain cells evaporated. Every last one of them disintegrated under the flaming pressure of his mouth.

His lips moved firmly over hers with barely restrained intensity, and her eyes fluttered closed. He savored her mouth, easing back and then diving in again, plucking at her lips and dragging the tip of his tongue along the inside of her mouth.

Her belly quaked, the breath from her lungs trembling in a rush through her nostrils. It had to be the most divine, most delicious feeling she'd ever experienced, and the sensations from his kiss reverberated between her thighs.

She ran her hands over his biceps to his shoulders, with the intent of pushing him away. But her fingers turned traitorous. They clamped on to his hard muscles, holding him tight. Refusing to let go.

Shamelessly, she kissed him back, angling her head, enjoying the warmth of his mouth and the way his muscled body pressed against hers. Both his hands clutched her hips and held her close to the contours of his body. His hot, firm body.

Her nerves went berserk; heat flushed her skin. Trembling, Ronnie wound her arms around his neck, falling into a deep pit of hunger as her senses erupted with erotic sensations.

She moaned, trembling fingers running through his wavy black hair. So thick. So soft. Head tipped back, she allowed him to deepen the kiss by sinking his tongue into her mouth. There was a second explosion of sensation when he cupped her small bottom in his big hands, squeezing her butt cheeks and hauling her tight against his hard thighs. His gripping fingers dragged her onto the tips of her shoes.

Her back met the wall, and soon a muscular thigh was sandwiched between her legs. The swell of something big and unyielding nudged her stomach, and she gasped. Nipples tightening. Head spinning.

Ronnie's eyes flew open at the shock of how quickly the kiss soared out of control, lasting way too long. That wasn't part of the plan. She'd expected something fast and quick.

He was still deeply engrossed in the intimate act, eyes closed. But panic filled her, and she pushed hard and shoved him away.

In the aftermath they stood a few feet apart, panting. Lungs grasping for air, chests heaving up and down. He appeared just as startled as she, a heaviness in his eyes that indicated lust. Longing.

She couldn't ever remember being kissed like that before. Sure, she'd felt desire, experienced passion. But this...this kiss possessed an all-consuming heat. Hot and intense. Not lukewarm. Not mediocre. It blew her mind.

"What was that?" Ronnie asked. The voice that came from her throbbing mouth startled her in its raspiness. She cleared her throat and stared at him, touching her neck where his fingers had caressed her skin. Her chest, back, and ass tingled though he never touched bare flesh, the phantom sensation of his caresses rippling up and down her spine. "You. Me. No way can that happen," she said.

"It just did." His own voice sounded raw and

husky.

"You drive me nuts."

"Apparently, I turn you on, too." His gaze dragged down her body and he bit his bottom lip, as if he wanted to take a bite out of her, too.

"But we get on each other's nerves."

"Our mouths don't."

Ronnie inhaled deeply and lifted her hands. "Okay, I paid my debt. So...we're done."

"You taste even better than I imagined. No way we're done, *mami*."

His tongue dragged along the outside of his lower lip, as if he were reliving the flavor of her mouth. The spot at the apex of her thighs quivered with longing.

"After that kiss, I won't be satisfied until I have all of you." He came at her again, and his mouth landed across hers, searing their lips together and making her knees as weak and wobbly as a newborn foal's.

She crooned with pleasure, clinging to him, kissing him with unrestrained desire. Throughout it all, one word shone like a lamp in the muddled darkness of her brain.

Finally.

Chapter Eleven

Ronnie rubbed her aching breasts against his chest, wishing her nipples were free and bare to experience full contact. Her entire being felt achy and inflamed, as if someone had set a match to gasoline and poured it into her veins.

Diego unzipped the jumpsuit and muttered something in Spanish when her half-naked body was revealed. She didn't know what he said and really didn't care. She only cared about the way his hands felt on her skin when he peeled the fabric past her shoulders and let it collapse into a puddle around her ankles.

He kissed her neck, his mouth providing a moist suction that wreaked havoc on the sensitive skin. She leaned into his lips and slid a hand between them. Cupping the hard steel between his legs, she shivered at the power and strength he exuded.

She wanted this. Longed for it. Had dreamed about it.

"Veronica." He groaned her name, with such ingrained agony that the sound elicited an answering moan from her.

Her fingers continued to caress him through the jeans as he unhooked her blue cotton bra at the back. The material fell away and bared her breasts. They were small, but more than enough to satisfy his mouth, as he dipped his head and plucked a pouty black nipple into his lips, sucking until she let out a pleading gasp. Hands on her waist, he circled the tip with his tongue and worked the nipple. Her head fell back to the wall, eyes closed as she gave herself over to his relentless oral assault.

His hands traced the curve of her spine, and her toes curled. Her dreams didn't nearly compare to this immeasurable pleasure. She never wanted him to stop touching her.

"Should I make you come on your back or on your stomach?" he asked.

Oh my goodness.

"Whatever you want." The words trembled on the way out.

A husky, masculine laugh followed, and Diego took his time kissing his way between her breasts and over the flat plane of her stomach.

Crouched before her, he dragged the yellow cotton panties down her legs, and for a split second Ronnie regretted not wearing matching underwear—or something lacy. When she dressed for work, she only thought about comfort and practicality. But Diego didn't seem to mind.

"*Hermosa.* I knew you'd have beautiful legs," he said, smoothing his hands up and down her thighs. He nipped at her skin and licked the crease of her hip.

He slid his hands down her legs, along the back of her knees, and down to her calves. Tiny tremors rippled over her skin wherever he touched.

Ronnie looked down at the top of his dark head and filled her fists with his hair, purring encouragingly as he continued to caress and mold her slender curves. When he flicked a thumb over her sensitized clit and kissed her wet mound, her knees buckled, almost giving way.

He removed her shoes and divested her of all clothes. Then he came to his feet and stood back to take a good look.

Diego's eyes smoldered with green fire. As if he wanted to devour her. And instead of being self-conscious, she felt empowered and sexy. Standing boldly, head held high, she put on a teasing show for him by squeezing her breasts together.

He growled low in his throat, lifted her off the ground in one swift movement, and dropped her atop the hood of the Corolla. Hastily, he removed his shirt, not bothering with the buttons—simply tugged it over his head and tossed it to the cement floor.

Her gaze sifted in amazement over his incredible body, riveted by the defined muscle, the dusting of dark hair over his golden skin. She splayed her fingers over the hard pecs and abs, and watched in fascination as his skin twitched under her touch.

She made a needy sound of longing and pulled Diego on top of her. His heavy body stretched over hers, pressing her into the cool surface of the car. She cooed as he explored her with his hands and mouth.

He whispered to her in Spanish, breathing softly onto her skin. And his tongue...oh his tongue did such delicious things. She twisted her head from left to right, moaning and gasping at the slow circle he made around her navel. When he traced moist, deliberate lines over and around her breasts, all she could do was helplessly strain closer.

"Please," she whimpered, unable to wait any longer. A year. A whole year she lusted after this man and denied her attraction for him. She could no longer deny. She could no longer run from the truth.

He heard her pleas and wasted no time shoving down his jeans and boxer briefs, which exposed his rigid erection to her greedy eyes. As he sheathed himself in a condom, Ronnie spread her legs. Exposing her body in a raw, unfiltered way. Offering him everything. All of herself.

His eyes became riveted to the moist cleft she laid open to him. His pupils dilated. His jaw tightened. And a growl rumbled in his chest.

They locked eyes before he fell between her thighs, coming down on her like a man possessed. He captured her hoarse cry in his mouth, and then pinning her arms to the cold metal, surged into her. There was no room for niceties. The drive of his body was hard and rough. Now that they were one, the pounding was mad, almost merciless in its intensity.

Her inner muscles loosened to allow him in further. It was barely enough. In a relentless fashion he pumped between her legs. Her back and ass skidded against the hard hood. Thrusting hips powered between her thighs and damn near pushed her through the metal to the systems underneath.

The sounds of their lovemaking filled the room. Heavy panting. The slap of skin against skin. Bathed in the bright overhead lights that shone down on them, Ronnie closed her eyes and surrendered to the tension tightening her loins.

The sounds she emitted consolidated into half whimpers and half groans. Gasping, pinned beneath him, she neared the climax. His strokes quickened and her body ripped apart as an orgasm wrenched through her body. She cried out, her body drawing taut, muscles tight and rigid.

"*Mierda.*"

Diego let out a powerful groan of his own before his body stiffened and he collapsed on top of her.

****

Ronnie bit back a moan of displeasure when Diego eased out of her arms. Sitting up, she brought her legs together in a more modest position.

She didn't know what to say. Here she was, naked on the hood of a car in her shop, and the last thing she wanted was to get dressed. Despite being satisfied, she wanted him again, as if a hungry, insatiable beast resided inside of her.

She glanced down and saw that he still wore his boots. He'd simply shoved down his pants in his haste to fuck her. Her breasts and loins ached at the evidence of such impatient lust.

Diego hadn't moved. He just stood there, looking at her.

"We should get out of here," she said.

"Not yet."

"Why not?" she whispered.

"Because I can do both."

"Both..?" Ronnie frowned, confused.

"Make you come on your back and your stomach."

Her clit throbbed, and she closed her eyes. Wanting it.

"Diego…"

He pushed her legs apart and stood between them. "Tell me you don't want it."

He nibbled at her ear and thumbed a nipple. She was still so sensitive and pulled back a little, but he wrapped a strong arm around her and took her mouth. There was no way she could refuse him. His kisses were too good and his touch already addictive. And the thought of him taking her from behind was too enticing to forego.

They made love again. Slower this time. When he pushed her onto her stomach, her breathing fractured in anticipation. The hot length of him pressed at the seam of her buttocks.

She heard the condom wrapper right before he pushed her legs wide.

"I don't think we're going to be done anytime soon," Diego whispered huskily. He kissed her shoulder blades and made a train of kisses down her spine.

"What do you mean?" Ronnie asked in a breathy voice. "You'll want to do this again?"

"Again." He filled her with his length, and she cried out at the exquisite feeling of being filled to capacity. "And again." He gave one hard pump of his hips and she cried out again, clawing at the smooth surface of the car. The cold metal on her raw, aching nipples contrasted with the warm kisses on her back.

And before long, Ronnie was screaming again, muscles taut, as another intense orgasm ravaged her body.

Chapter Twelve

Ronnie couldn't get enough of Diego. Actually, they couldn't get enough of each other.

For the most part they kept their hooking up low-key, but the men in the shop picked up on the relationship, mainly because of Diego's drop-ins during the day, and every so often she and he sat in the parking lot on the tailgate of his truck, eating lunch together.

Her employees teased her mercilessly, making kissing sounds and reminding her of how much Diego annoyed her in the beginning.

"Live and learn," was all she said and shrugged.

Almost every evening right before she closed the shop, he sauntered in and joined her in the office while she wrapped up paperwork. Each time she watched him walk through the door, she bit her lip and admired the slow, sexy walk he seemed to have mastered. No other man moved like him, with such casual confidence. And all the while, the memory of hot sex licked between her legs.

For their sexcapades they used the desk, or the only empty spot on the wall that didn't have a piece of furniture pushed against it. She liked touching him. Every single part of him. If he wore a D&M Towing hat, Ronnie pushed it off his head and ran her fingers through his hair. At the earliest opportunity, she kissed his neck and slipped a hand under his shirt to touch warm skin and hard muscle.

But Diego was more than a handsome face and tight body. The similarities in their personalities attracted her to him, too. They were both very stubborn. They both worked hard to make their businesses succeed and wanted happy employees. Both enjoyed sports, although she questioned some of his choices in who he chose to root for.

They also liked to needle each other. His favorite thing to do was prop his feet on her desk. No matter how many times she told him not to. A surefire way to get Diego to do something was to tell him not to do it.

Ronnie was in the middle of writing checks for bills when Diego entered the office. "How about we grab a bite to eat after work tonight?"

She finished signing her name and looked up. The sight of him never failed to have the same effect each and every time. She caught her breath, and her heartbeat accelerated.

She couldn't ever remember experiencing such breathless excitement in the presence of any man before. Every day she looked forward to seeing him, and when he went out on a call, she counted the minutes until his truck pulled into the parking lot.

"You want to go out?"

They'd never been out together. Their clandestine hookups remained restricted to the confines of the property.

"I have a taste for Chinese food."

"I could go for Chinese," Ronnie said.

"Good. I'll drive."

She walked around the desk, but instead of moving, Diego remained in the same position, blocking the door.

"Are you going to move?" she asked.

"Are you going to say excuse me?"

"I thought you had a taste for Chinese food?"

"I do. I have a taste for Veronica, too."

He cupped her chin and gazed down into her eyes. Now that he had permission to touch her, he seemed to want to do so all the time. Her insides danced in anticipation. Every time he touched her she reacted in a visceral, instinctual way. The most innocuous of contact, such as placing a hand on her shoulder, caused her shoulder to tense. It wasn't that he bothered her. It was just that he was a man and she was a woman, and whenever he touched her, she remembered that.

Diego kissed her slowly, as if he relished the taste of her mouth. Ronnie melted against him, and his hardening erection prodded her stomach.

"You've awakened *el Gigante*," he said.

She laughed softly and playfully slapped his chest. He referred to his penis as the Sleeping Giant, or simply, *el Gigante* for short.

"Are you going to feed me or not?" She leaned into his sturdy chest.

He groaned and gave a quick suck of her neck. "I'll feed you. You're too cranky when you're hungry." He strolled off.

Something else they had in common. "Like you aren't!" she shot back.

Instead of driving both vehicles, they agreed to take Diego's truck the few miles to the restaurant.

He unlocked the passenger door, and when she started climbing into the truck, he placed a hand below her elbow.

Ronnie's stomach gave way and she froze. She looked back at him.

A frown grooved his forehead. "Is something wrong?"

No stranger to hoisting heavy objects in the garage or climbing in and out of trucks, she didn't need any help. But his strong, steady hand was surprisingly reassuring. She couldn't possibly explain to him why such a simple gesture meant so much.

"No. Everything's fine."

She climbed up and his hand at her back helped her settle on the seat. The truck still carried that new-car smell. The supple leather seat cupped her derriere, and the wood grain interior shone like newly polished stone.

She watched him walk around to the driver's side, his profile strong, his stride long and confident.

Before starting the vehicle, he turned a quizzical gaze on her. "You sure everything's okay?"

"Yes. Can't wait to eat."

****

Red lanterns hung from the red ceiling of the Chinese restaurant. The hostess seated Diego and Ronnie in a booth and took their drink orders. Then she left.

"What are you having?" Ronnie asked, reviewing

the menu.

"I can tell you what I'd like to have," Diego said, a slow smile coming over his face.

Heat surged in her blood. Whenever he looked at her with those sleepy, heat-filled eyes, she knew exactly what he wanted.

"I'm talking about what's on the menu," she said, tapping the laminated paper.

"Oh, what's on the menu..." As if he didn't know what she'd meant.

"Yes, what are you having?"

He snapped the menu shut and set it aside. "Mongolian beef."

Ronnie trailed her gaze through the chicken and seafood options. "I'll have the orange chicken. I haven't eaten that in a while."

She placed her menu on top of his. "So I see you sold the Corolla."

A college-aged-looking young man had driven it off the lot late last week.

Diego nodded. "I need you to take a look at a Lexus, too. I should be able to make a pretty penny off that one."

Ronnie squeezed lemon juice into her glass of water. "What's wrong with it?"

"Nothing, so far as I can tell, but I need you to give it the twenty-five-point inspection."

"When do you think—"

The waitress chose that moment to come forward. Dressed in a traditional Chinese costume, including chopsticks in her hair, she smiled pleasantly and asked for their order. They told her their choices, but after she left, Ronnie didn't get a chance to resume the conversation because a female police officer walked up to the table.

"Hello, Diego," she said. Her honey-blonde hair was pulled into a neat up do under her hat.

Almost imperceptibly, Diego's body tensed, which signaled to Ronnie right away that there was more to their acquaintance than simple friendship. Not to mention the officer practically ate him up with her eyes. Otherwise, he didn't react much to the woman's presence,

"Good to see you again," she said.

"Good to see you, too." He didn't make any introductions, and after an awkward pause, the officer wished them a good night and walked away.

"What were you saying?" Diego sat casually in the chair, looking across the table at her as if he hadn't skipped introducing the two women. Rather than call him on it, Ronnie behaved as if nothing unusual had occurred.

"When do you want me to look at the Lexus?" she asked.

"As soon as you can fit me in."

Their food arrived, and they dug in. The conversation turned to sports, and he razzed her about the fact that the Hawks had been eliminated from the playoffs. They ended up in a spirited argument that took her mind off the lack of introduction with the police officer, when another woman wearing a figure-hugging black dress, which could only be described as glued to her thick frame, stopped at the table. Ronnie didn't see how there was any way she got into the outfit without the aid of grease and an advanced pulley system.

"Hello Diego. I thought that was you." She smiled at them both, but her eyes quickly shifted back to

Diego.

Before he could reply, Ronnie stuck out her hand. The woman's eyebrows shot up in surprise.

"Ronnie. Nice to meet you."

"Nice to meet you. I'm Sandra." They shook hands.

"Diego, I hope we'll see you again real soon."

"You will."

He returned to eating his food, and Sandra sashayed away.

"How do you know Sandra?" Ronnie asked, shoving chicken around on her plate.

"She works in the front office at Flower Power Plaza. I submitted a proposal to handle their towing." His voice sounded suspiciously neutral. To Ronnie's mind, overly so.

"I see. Did you sleep with her?"

His fork clattered to the plate when he dropped it. "Don't—"

"Don't what? Ask you questions about the women you're screwing since you don't seem very inclined to introduce them after you're done?"

Why was she so upset? Those women didn't matter, did they? Sure, she looked like a stick drawing next to their curvaceous forms, but Diego wanted her, Ronnie. He was sleeping with *her*.

For the moment.

In another month, maybe less, she'd be like the police officer and the front-office worker. Unworthy of introduction, treated to a simple hello and forced to dismiss herself at his lack of interest.

"Whatever you're thinking—"

"I'm not thinking anything," Ronnie snapped, glaring at him across the table.

She couldn't eat another morsel. If she ate one more bite, she may puke everything onto the table. Ronnie pushed the plate to the side and sipped her water.

"Are you ready to go?" he asked in a stilted voice.

"Yes."

A few minutes later, the waitress reappeared, and he called her over. She packed up Diego's dinner, but Ronnie passed on hers.

They rode in utter silence to their workplace. Ronnie sat with her arms folded and stared out the window. As soon as he stopped the truck, she hopped out. He followed her to her vehicle, but when she tried to open the door, he came right behind her and held it shut, a strong forearm parallel to the corner of her eye.

"You're very quiet."

She wanted to argue but didn't want to argue, worried about rocking the tenuous boat of their...She didn't even know what they were doing. She felt possessive when she had no right to. They certainly weren't in a relationship, and two weeks in was too soon to make demands.

She folded her arms. "You know a lot of women."

"Not a lot."

"Hah."

"Look at me."

She refused to turn around.

He lowered his lips beside her ear. "Those women are my past."

Don't do it. Don't ask.

"And what am I?" Her brain and mouth were not in sync.

"What do you want to be?" he asked.

She turned to face him.

"Tell me what you want. You've spent enough time with men to know we don't do that mind-reading bullshit."

She stared at the streetlight over his shoulder. "I don't want to just...hook up."

"So what do you want?"

"Why are you trying to make me say it?"

"Because if you don't say what you want, that's a surefire way to make sure you never get it."

"Fine! I don't only want to screw in my office after work. I don't want to grab a bite to eat. I want...I want to make actual plans and go on dates. I want to be courted."

She was an emotional wreck. Tension burned her throat and her eyes dodged his. She awaited his response in the strained silence.

"We can do that."

The tension in her throat eased, and her gaze found his.

"I thought *el Gigante* was all you needed, but I guess not." He smiled a brilliant smile.

Ronnie shoved him away, but he bounced back, closer than before. His forearm flattened on the truck and brought him all up on her.

"See how easy that was? You tell me what you want and you get it." He used a forefinger to tilt up her chin and forced her to look into his eyes. "We did things a little backwards. Of course it's all *el Gigante*'s fault because he waited a whole year before he made any progress with you, and he was so excited when we finally kissed he wasted no time going from first base to sliding into home."

"Stop talking about your penis like it's a person."

"Trust me, he has a mind of his own," Diego said in a solemn voice.

Ronnie arched a brow and in return he flashed a lazy smile. "Saturday night I'm taking you on a date. We'll go to a nice restaurant for dinner and do something else. Something different."

"You don't have to..."

Now it was his turn to raise a brow.

Ronnie giggled, suddenly giddy with excitement. "Okay, I'm lying."

Diego traced a finger along her jaw. "I better go before *el Gigante* makes an appearance. He's starting to get a little unruly in this parking lot, watching those gorgeous lips of yours smile."

Ronnie stood on tiptoe and dragged his bottom lip into her mouth. Diego groaned and kissed her, swiping the tip of his tongue in a quick motion across her upper lip.

"Tell him I'll see him later this week," Ronnie whispered.

"I'll do that."

She lifted into her vehicle, but Diego angled into the cabin before she closed the door.

"Just so you know, you're nothing like those other women." He held her gaze for a minute, as if to drive the point home, and then he closed the door and walked away.

Chapter Thirteen

Some of Ronnie's fondest memories consisted of the time she'd spent with her two male cousins every summer. During the school year, they were busy with after school events and weekend activities, but the boys packed in plenty during the summer months, and Ronnie was right there with them.

While their sister Anika spent time with girls her own age, playing with dolls and experimenting with makeup, Ronnie and the boys climbed trees, fished, and went tubing down the Chattahoochee River. The boys eventually moved away to pursue lives outside the state, but oddly enough, Anika and Ronnie had developed a bond much closer than when they were children.

For that reason, Ronnie confided in her cousin about the relationship with Diego and told her about the upcoming date. As soon as she heard the details, Anika dropped everything and came over right away.

Anika dressed well, always. She knew how to

accessorize any outfit with the right brooch, belt, or scarf. Hair and makeup, always flawless. Even dressed casually as she was today, in a purple velour jogging suit and her hair in a ponytail that hung between her shoulder blades, she looked ready for a magazine spread. She had the "it" factor, and that was why Ronnie needed her.

Legs crossed, her cousin sat on the bed in the sparsely furnished bedroom containing a queen bed, two dressers, and a bedside table. Never one for fancy decorations or frilly designs, Ronnie examined the room with a critical eye. A splash of paint wouldn't hurt. Nothing too extreme—something neutral but warmer than the stark white currently on the walls.

A little more color would be nice, too, like the orange gingham bed linens and matching curtains and decorative pillows she'd seen online. The entire set was on clearance and moderately priced, sitting in the online cart, waiting for her to click *Buy*.

"Now I know why you didn't give Edgar a chance. You already have a man."

"I don't have a man." Ronnie made a mental note to get the small white lamp from the attic. Hopefully, it still worked.

She dropped to her haunches in the closet and removed a shoebox that contained a pair of gold sandals she bought a long time ago and never thought she'd wear. She didn't even know why she'd bought them. She seldom wore heels, but the simple elegance of the design intrigued her and she'd picked them up, thinking that maybe one day she'd have occasion to wear them.

"You're sleeping with him," Anika pointed out.

"We're not doing labels," Ronnie said. "We're just

hanging out."

"Uh-huh." Anika smiled knowingly, her eyes alight with excitement and possibilities.

Ronnie sighed. "You're hopeless."

Anika loved romantic comedies and believed in love at first sight. There was no getting through to her. If she could, she'd have Ronnie walking down the aisle to Diego within the next thirty days.

He and Ronnie were having sex, but still getting to know each other. This was the hard part about seeing someone, and why she preferred terms like "hanging out." Ambiguity allowed both parties to walk away with their pride intact, and minimized the fallout if the relationship didn't last. When you held onto someone—took ownership of them with labels like my boyfriend or my man—it made walking away dreadfully complicated.

"What's in the box?" Anika asked.

"These." Ronnie lifted the lid on the shoe box and exposed the three-inch heels nestled inside.

"Nice," Anika said. "We might need to go shopping, unless you have something cute to wear. You'd drown in anything I loan you because...well, these hips and these breasts are no joke." She patted her hips and they both laughed.

"I have something that could work." Ronnie went back to the closet and pulled out a blue and gold striped tent dress. "What do you think?"

Anika tilted her head to the side. "Mmm, nice. Do you know where you're going?"

"He didn't say."

"What else do you have?"

"Not much." A few more skirts and dresses, none of which seemed adequate. The majority of her wardrobe consisted of pants and shirts. "Oh, wait," she murmured to herself.

In the very back, a sleeveless orange jersey dress hung on a hanger. She'd bought it on the spur of the moment after seeing it in a store window. Ronnie took it into the bedroom, the tag dangling under the arm, and held it up for Anika's inspection. "What about this?"

Eyes wide, Anika gasped. She leaped from the bed. Running her fingers over the clingy material, she said, "I love it."

Ronnie did, too. She'd never had an occasion to wear it before, but now seemed like the perfect time.

"You'll have to wear a thong with this or you'll have lines."

Ronnie wrinkled her nose. "Couldn't I—"

"Thong."

"All right, all right."

"Next, makeup." Anika placed her hands on her hips and studied Ronnie. "Do you want to go heavy or light?"

Ronnie touched a hand to her face. "Not too heavy. I need to be able to reapply it when you're not here."

"We probably need to make a trip to the mall."

"We don't need to do that," Ronnie said.

"Listen, we need the right tools to work on your face."

"A trip is really not necessary."

Ronnie walked over to the larger dresser and pulled open the two top drawers. She collected lipsticks, and one drawer contained tubes in almost every shade imaginable from various brands. From Revlon to Iman, she'd purchased different colors to see which best matched her skin tone.

Her cousin came up behind her and gasped at the collection.

The next drawer contained an assortment of foundation, mascara, brushes, eyeliner—the works.

"I practically had to beg you to wear makeup when we went to dinner at Shula's," Anika said.

"Makeup is a hassle to put on. Lipstick always feels heavy and unnatural on my mouth, and it's not as if I ever go anywhere that warrants wearing makeup."

"Just going outside warrants wearing makeup. As my mother always says, 'Never leave the house without your face on.'"

They giggled at her spot-on impersonation.

"Once you get used to wearing makeup, you won't even remember it's on." Anika ran her hands over the tubes of lipsticks, and they clacked against each other. "Some of them haven't even been opened yet."

"I know." She'd always felt strangely awkward wearing makeup, and it was so much easier to get dressed and go out when she didn't have to worry about "putting on her face." Whereas some women took an hour or longer to get ready, she only needed thirty minutes, tops, which included a shower.

"Oh, honey, we're about to have some fun," Anika said, a gleam in her eye.

They carried a handful of the products into the bathroom where better lighting allowed Anika to experiment on Ronnie's face. First, she put on the mascara and demonstrated how to dust on powder to take away the shine. They tried bright colors on her lips, starting with fuchsia, then shifted to more neutral tones in the brown family, and finished with a dark purple that appeared almost black. Over an hour later, they ended the session with a wine red and overlaid it with lip gloss—giving Ronnie's mouth a full, attractive sheen.

"What do you think?" Anika asked, standing back and admiring her handiwork.

Ronnie inspected her reflection, checking out the thicker-looking lashes, the even, matte finish of her skin, and the plump attractiveness of her mouth. "I like it. I don't look like I'm trying too hard, but it looks like I made an effort."

"You're all set." Anika grinned, rubbing her hands together like an evil scientist from an old B-movie. "Diego must be really something."

"Why do you say that?" Ronnie continued to examine her face in the mirror.

"You've never, ever gone through all this trouble for a man."

Heart racing, Ronnie touched a hand to her face and stared at her reflection, barely recognizing the person looking back at her. She couldn't dismiss Anika's observation.

Because what she'd said was absolutely true.

Chapter Fourteen

Diego arrived at the Taylor house in a foul mood. The conversation with Loisa on the ride over had made him uneasy. They'd argued, and he vainly kept the irritation out of his voice when he deflected questions about his plans for the night and with whom. A crisp "goodbye" finally shut her down, and he hung up to at least be civil when he arrived to pick up Ronnie.

He pressed the doorbell, straightened the striped gray and blue tie on his white shirt, and waited. After a few moments, Ronnie appeared in the doorway, and the anger disappeared.

Struck silent, all he could do was stare.

She looked different, breathtaking, standing with the light from the entryway behind her. Right away he noticed her hair was neater, as if she'd recently had it trimmed. Light makeup and lipstick in a dark wine color covered her lips and gave them a lusher appearance.

"Hi," she said. Unbelievably, she appeared nervous, hands folded in front of her, waiting for him to speak.

Meanwhile, Diego fought to pull air into his tightened lungs. He wanted to skip the rest of the evening and take her back to his house.

"*Hermosa, mami,*" he murmured, unable to resist dragging his eyes down the form-fitting dress to her feet, clad in a pair of gold heels several inches higher than the shoes she normally wore.

She practically glowed, the outfit showing off her svelte body—slender but curvaceous hips, small and high breasts, and toned arms. The sleeveless orange dress played beautifully against the color of her dark, burnished skin.

Her brown eyes beamed with pure pleasure.

"Are you ready to go?" Diego asked, mind racing. He needed to get his libido under control, or soon he'd be insisting they skip the rest of the evening so he could take her back to his place.

"Let me grab my purse."

She ducked into the house and he stepped onto the threshold to wait for her. When she returned, she wore a tiny purse wrapped around her wrist and a pair of small earrings. As she walked toward him, a faint smile graced her lips, and his eyes were drawn to the modest switch of her hips with each step.

Damn. He was a lucky man.

"Nugget, you heading out?" someone called from upstairs.

"Yes."

"Hang on."

Ronnie groaned. "That's my father. He wants to meet you." She lifted her gaze to the top of the stairs.

"No problem."

With a voice like he'd heard, Diego expected to see a giant of a man. The person descending the stairs didn't appear to be much taller than Ronnie, yet somehow managed to be an imposing figure. Frowning, the older man assessed him through a pair of glasses wearing an old blue and white robe that clearly implied he did not need to impress anyone—he was the one who needed to be impressed.

"So you're Diego Molina."

"Yes, sir. Nice to meet you." Diego extended his hand. Being polite, respectful, and forthright were the best ways to impress any father, no matter the age of his daughter.

"Ezekiel Taylor."

Both men pumped hands in a firm handshake.

"Daddy, don't embarrass me," Ronnie said from the corner of her mouth, in a loud whisper.

Ezekiel didn't react, as if Ronnie never said a word. "So you're from Cuba?"

"Yes, but I lived in Miami most of my life before moving to Atlanta a few years ago."

"I guess that's why you speak such good English."

"Oh my god," Ronnie murmured, covering her face.

The corner of Diego's mouth twitched. "That's probably why, yes."

"Your parents still in Miami?"

Pain surged in the back of his throat and Diego swallowed with difficulty. "No, sir. Both of my parents are dead."

"I'm sorry to hear that." Ezekiel adjusted the glasses lower on his nose. "You a religious man?"

"Daddy, please."

"I believe in God."

"You're welcome to come to church with me any Sunday. Both of you." He looked pointedly at Ronnie and she pursed her lips.

He viewed Diego over the top of the glasses, gauging his response to the next question. "What are your intentions toward my daughter?"

"Okay, that's enough." Ronnie stepped between them.

"I'm not done," her father protested.

"Yes, you are. Bye."

"Wait a minute—"

"Good night, Daddy." Ronnie shoved Diego out the door.

"Good night, Mr. Taylor."

The door closed behind them and Ronnie rushed to the truck. After Diego helped her in, he hopped in on his side. Ezekiel stood in the window with the curtain drawn aside, watching them.

"Oh my goodness, just go." Ronnie sighed.

Diego chuckled and backed out of the driveway. Her father was quite a character.

"You have a great dad," Diego said.

"I have an overprotective father."

"Has he always been that way?"

"Always. Surprisingly, worse now that I'm an adult."

They drove in silence for a while.

"His behavior may seem like a bad thing, but it's not." Diego barely saw the road ahead for the bitterness twisting inside him. "At least you know he loves you."

****

Ronnie was bored out of her mind.

Well-dressed patrons perused the abstract paintings and mixed-media sculptures displayed at various intervals around the room. A quiet hum of conversation comingled with the soft jazz coming through hidden speakers.

Of course plenty of people would enjoy an evening at the High Museum, an elegant place located in Midtown. The art was certainly...interesting—the most polite adjective Ronnie could think of to describe it. She certainly was no connoisseur of art, but if she did buy paintings she'd prefer that they were of actual images she recognized.

Tipping her head to the left and then to the right, she examined a giant painting—a hodgepodge of red, yellow, and vibrant blue against a backdrop of black. How could this be considered art? The image resembled a project her five-year-old self could have created, something her father would have proudly pinned to the refrigerator door with a magnet.

She felt a pang of guilt for not enjoying herself more. Standing a few feet away, Diego stared up at one of the paintings, but she couldn't read his expression.

Is he really enjoying this?

She smothered a yawn behind her hand.

Maybe. What did she know? As much time as she spent around men, they were still an enigma.

"Gorgeous, isn't it?" a man with long silver hair to her right whispered.

"Absolutely," Ronnie whispered back, because whispering seemed to be appropriate etiquette. If she gave her true opinion, she'd reveal her lack of refinement and probably offend the man. She stifled another yawn and smiled politely.

"This piece was done by a local artist. Toro. Have you heard of him?" He leaned in, his attention dropping to her breasts before quickly returning to her eyes.

"No, I'm not familiar with—"

"You ready to eat?" Diego had come up behind her and splayed his fingers across her hip. Warmth oozed over her skin.

"Excuse me." The older man cleared his throat and walked away.

"Yes, I'm ready to eat."

Ronnie smiled up Diego, who watched the man with a hard set to his jaw.

Was he jealous?

The comfortable jersey fabric of the dress felt soft against her skin, but stretched taut over her torso, hips, and thighs. She didn't have the type of bodacious body that turned heads under normal circumstances, but she did notice she'd caught the eye of several men over the course of the evening.

She'd be a liar if she didn't admit a small part of her enjoyed the attention, but an even bigger part of her felt thrilled that Diego might be a little jealous.

They exited the main hall and walked outside where the valet quickly retrieved his truck. Once on the road, Diego sent a quick glance in her direction. "What did you think?"

"It was nice," Ronnie replied, keeping her voice neutral.

Diego flipped the left indicator. "How is business at the shop? You mentioned once that revenues were down."

Ronnie plucked at the hem of her dress. "Not much has changed. I have to figure out how to increase business."

Diego reduced speed when they neared the Fox Theatre. Pedestrians crowded the streets, having left a live performance only minutes before. Traffic slowed to a crawl.

"Advertising hasn't helped?" he asked.

Ronnie shook her head. "We've been in a slump for months." She sighed. "How about you?"

"Steady. Better since we won the contract to tow at Flower Power Plaza."

"What? Congratulations!"

He laughed, a throaty, contented sound that spiked warmth in her chest. His laughter, his smile, his energy always sent a charge through her.

"I'll have to hire another employee soon."

They smiled at each other. She was genuinely happy for him, if a little envious.

She simply didn't have the marketing savvy to generate business, but she was a helluva mechanic, and so were her guys. In an industry where unethical technicians tarnished the reputation of all in the field, they conducted business in an honest and dependable manner. She wished she knew of a way to convey that message to customers and bring more business to the shop.

Diego pulled into the parking lot of the restaurant, a posh eatery located in a converted warehouse that served up an eclectic blend of Asian and Latin cuisine. "I heard this place has great tapas," he said.

Attendants on either side opened their doors, and Ronnie slid out.

She remembered when the restaurant opened a few months ago, but had never come by. She had a big appetite and wasn't a fan of tapas. Tonight, however, she chose to keep an open mind.

"Can't wait to try the food," she said, injecting enthusiasm into her voice.

A host dressed in black seated them near a window, where they could look out at the city street. The sound of silverware hitting plates and the gentle hum of dinner chatter filled the dining room. Food at the surrounding tables looked delicious, presented on small ceramic plates. Meats nestled in thick sauces, the vibrant pink of shrimp on a bed of lettuce, and miniature tacos with chopped cilantro sprinkled over them like a garnish. But the portion sizes couldn't possibly fill her, much less Diego, and a glance at the menu showed such exorbitant prices, he'd have to take out a small loan to pay for the five plates she expected to order just to satisfy her appetite.

"What made you choose this restaurant?" Ronnie asked. The candlelight flicked over the chiseled lines of his face.

"A friend recommended it."

His gaze remained on the menu, and Ronnie observed his stiff posture and the way his brows sank low over his eyes.

"Too bad this place doesn't serve hamburgers," she said in a conversational tone, throwing out the joke to test his reaction. "I could go for a juicy hamburger with grilled onions, cheese, and bacon." Simply mentioning the combination made her mouth water and stomach do anticipatory somersaults.

"Yeah." Diego scratched his jaw, flipping to the back of the menu, and an even deeper frown of consternation marred his forehead.

On a hunch, Ronnie leaned across the table and said, "There's a cool movie playing at the drive-in tonight."

His gaze shot across the table, surprise in his eyes. He slowly lowered the menu. "You want to go to the drive-in?"

Ronnie tried to gauge his interest, but couldn't quite.

"Tell the truth. Do you really want to stay here?"

A slow smile spread over his face. "Let me guess, this isn't your type of place?"

"I'm seriously trying to figure out why you brought me here," she admitted.

He laughed, and folded his arms at the edge of the table. "Seems I received bad advice. Would you believe I was told it was something you might enjoy?"

"Did the same person suggest the art exhibit?"

"Unfortunately, yes."

"A woman made those suggestions?"

"Uh-huh."

"Do you even realize who you're talking to right now?"

One corner of his mouth lifted into a sideways grin, one part cute and one part sexy. "I'm starting to figure it out," he said.

The waiter came over with pen in hand and greeted them both, showing plenty of teeth as he launched into a listing of the night's specials—the usual spiel from waiters and waitresses in every nice restaurant she'd ever been to—voice barely louder than the murmurs around them. He finished with, "What can I start you off with to drink?"

"We're not eating after all," Diego said, holding out the menu.

The server took it. "Is something the matter?" His face was tinged with concern.

Diego immediately tried to put his mind at ease. "Nothing's wrong. We just decided that we want to go somewhere else." He looked across the table at Ronnie. "Let's get out of here."

She handed her menu to the waiter and jumped up from the chair.

****

Diego should have known Ronnie was not like other women and shouldn't have listened to his friend's wife, who'd given him very bad advice. She couldn't have been more wrong.

They sat in the cab of the truck, Ronnie with her bare feet curled beneath her, and the FM radio tuned to the station broadcasting the sound of the movie, the latest superhero flick, with lots of explosions and CGI. They wolfed down greasy cheeseburgers, chili hotdogs, and fries. He sipped on a Coke, and she drank a Full Moon lager.

He didn't have to pretend he liked Beethoven when he preferred Led Zeppelin. He didn't have to pretend he liked foie gras when he'd rather eat hush puppies. He could be himself.

Only one problem marred the otherwise perfect end to the evening. Ronnie squirted ketchup all over her fries instead of squeezing it off to the side and dipping them into the condiment.

"There's something wrong with you," he said, pointing. "No normal person eats ketchup with fries like that."

She stabbed the fries with a fork and cut her eyes at him. "Smothered in ketchup is my preference, and there's no better way to eat them." She shoved four fries into her mouth and wrinkled her nose at him.

He laughed. Damn, she had an appetite. He

couldn't figure out where she put all that food, but it was refreshing to watch a woman eat and enjoy herself, without talk about diets and counting calories. They ordered the same items, but she didn't try to be cute by picking at her meal, which amazed him because she was a tiny little thing, so small he could practically tuck her under one arm and carry her away.

"Did you see that!" Ronnie exclaimed, pointing at the screen.

He didn't have a clue what she was looking at. He was too busy looking at her.

She was truly amazing. Wearing a T-shirt and jeans, she held her own in a room full of men. For a night out, she'd donned heels and put on a dress that showed off her sexy shape, but was completely satisfied with hamburgers and fries.

Diego was starting to think he might have found the ideal woman.

Chapter Fifteen

Diego didn't actually make plans for Ronnie to return home with him, but by the time the credits rolled, they both knew she would. It was just understood as the next step, and when he mentioned spending the night, she agreed.

Ronnie called Ezekiel to let him know she'd be staying out all night, and Diego smiled as she whispered fiercely to her father about being a grown woman.

He lived on a quiet cul-de-sac in a ranch on a basement. They pulled into the two-car garage, which at the moment could only accommodate his truck because one side was filled with furniture and stacked boxes. Shelves lined the walls, holding tools and gardening supplies.

Diego came around to the passenger side of the vehicle and intended to help Ronnie down. He placed both hands on her waist to do so, but instead ended up lifting her into his arms. Her soft body felt perfect against him.

"Hey," he whispered.

"Hey," she whispered back.

That smile and the beauty in those chocolate eyes melted his boxers.

Her head came down toward his. A charge pulsed through his blood when their lips met and her fingers delved into his hair. He loved when she ran her fingers through his hair, rubbing the tips along his scalp in a soothing massage over the crown and nape. He looked forward to her touch and could barely refrain from sitting at her shop all day, every day. The only reason he didn't was because they both had work to do.

She captured his face in her palms and moved her mouth across his in a gentle motion. A moan rumbled in his chest at the delicate texture of the kiss. The arms wrapped under her bottom tightened.

They barely made it to the bed. The distance from the kitchen almost proved too long a stretch in the heat of the moment. But Diego endured, carrying her through the silent house to his bedroom in the back.

Still touching, still kissing, he placed her on the bed and then turned on a lamp. His hungry gaze watched the shadows play over her dark brown skin. As he came down on her, her eyes fluttered closed. Her long lashes rested against her cheeks.

Diego pushed his hands beneath her dress, shoving the jersey fabric up to her thighs. Her legs were on display for him—bare, beautiful. He slid the scrap of fabric past her knees and tossed it to the floor. Her legs fell apart, and he pressed a soft, moist kiss to her sex. Her body jerked at the contact and she clutched the sheets, gasping. Encouraged, Diego braced his arms on either side of her thighs and maneuvered his tongue in a more probing motion around her moist clit. Damn, how he loved the smell and taste of her.

Ronnie shivered and whispered his name.

Grasping him by the hair, she dragged him up and they kissed. He transferred the flavor from between her legs into her mouth. Their kiss was warm and sweet. As always, he couldn't stop kissing her. He tried, but each time he trailed kisses down her cheek or over the arch in her throat, he was drawn back to the deliciousness of her mouth. So good. So exquisite.

Diego stroked between her thighs and pinched her clit. Her hips lifted off the bed, silently pleading for his possession. He was anxious, too, and didn't want to wait any longer. He unzipped and quickly sheathed in a condom. Lifting her hips with one hand, he pushed inside of her with ease, her body wet and welcoming.

He dived back into her mouth with his tongue. They kissed hungrily, hurriedly, as he continued to thrust his length inside of her. She arched off the mattress, panting into his mouth, clawing at his back. At that moment he realized he'd not even removed his jacket, so impatient to get close to her that he'd simply dropped his pants and taken her.

The sex between them could be like that. Sometimes slow and sensuous. Other times quick and fierce.

Heat crawled up his neck and pressure built in his loins, the pleasure of sinking into her warm, wet heat almost unbearable. His hand drifted between them, and he thumbed her clit, pushing her more quickly to orgasm.

She gasped, lips parted and eyes wide, as if she couldn't believe it. She cried out as the orgasm ricocheted through her body. Her feminine muscles trembled around his shaft in bursts of spasms.

That was when he lost the fight to hold back. His butt muscles tight, he unleashed in the condom and groaned, struggling to stay aright but failing miserably. He collapsed onto her and pressed his face into her neck.

He inhaled his two favorite scents in the world. Vanilla's earthy aroma from the light moisturizer she sprayed on her hair, and the enticing sweetness of her hibiscus-scented soap.

"Welcome to my home. *Bienvenida a mi casa.*"

Ronnie laughed breathlessly. "It's nice."

"You like it?" he asked, lifting his head.

"From what I've seen so far, the ceiling is great," she deadpanned.

He chuckled and pressed his face into her covered breasts. He kissed the left one, and the nipple pressed against the material.

"Have I told you how much I like this dress?" he asked, looking down at the way their bodies were joined and the dress shoved up to her waist. He liked the fact that most of the time she wore clothes that hid her body. That she wore this outfit for him aroused a sense of masculine pride in him and stroked his ego.

"You mentioned it," she said.

He eased out of her and went to the adjoining bathroom to discard the condom. When he came back, she was sitting up and had pulled the dress down. Without a word, Diego helped her from the bed and undressed them slowly.

They didn't make love again. They burrowed under the covers and he wrapped her in his arms. They should have done this sooner. She belonged here in his bed like this.

He cupped the back of her head, caressing the soft, tight coils of her hair with his fingers.

"Good night," she whispered.

"Good night." He kissed her forehead and drifted off to sleep.

****

Ronnie awoke slowly in the lamp-lit room, disoriented by the unfamiliar surroundings. The big bed was in the middle of a surprisingly neat but masculine bedroom decorated with a padded leather headboard and gray and white bed linens.

During the night, she and Diego shifted, and now she lay on her back with his arm thrown across her waist. She tried to ease from under him.

His arm tensed and he looked at her through slits in his eyes. "Am I too heavy?" he asked.

"No, but I need to get out. I'm thirsty."

"I'll get you something to drink." He groaned as he rolled onto his back. Ronnie set her hand on his chest and stopped him.

"I can get it myself. I know where the kitchen is."

His head dropped back to the pillow. "Hurry back.'

She left the bed and grabbed his sleeveless white undershirt from the floor. She slipped it over her head. It bore the scent of his cologne—a musky fragrance with spicy undertones—and his own natural scent.

She flipped the switch in the hallway and squinted when the light came on. Photos lined the wall, and she studied them as she advanced to the kitchen.

In one, a younger version of Diego, with a beard and short cut low to his scalp, stood with his arms around a short, older woman. Based on the similarity in their features, he assumed she was his mother. They stood in front of a house, smiling.

Another framed photo showed him and another young man who could be his twin, if not for the fact that he appeared to be younger. His brother, probably. With their skinny bare chests on display, they lounged against the hood of a Chevy, trying to look cool. Neither one looked older than sixteen.

Several pictures contained a little girl with laughing brown eyes and a bright smile. One in particular struck Ronnie, and she paused to examine the photo more closely. The little girl looked about three in this one, sitting atop Diego's shoulders and laughing heartily. They both were, and so was the woman holding onto his arm. She reminded Ronnie of the actress/singer Cristina Milian—very photogenic, with a light brown complexion, long, shiny hair, and dark eyes. Gorgeous, really.

Someone or something had tickled them, and the photographer caught them at the right moment to capture their joy and the uncanny resemblance between Diego and the child—not obvious in the photos of the little girl by herself. She was the spitting image of him right then, with their mouths half open, eyes squinted almost shut in the throes of laughter.

Did Diego have a daughter?

Frowning to herself, Ronnie went into the kitchen. The refrigerator contained juice, water, and some fruit, and a covered dish of what looked like leftovers.

She poured herself a glass of water, and while she

drank it, something furry rubbed against her leg. She gasped and jumped back, sloshing water on the floor. A black and white cat looked up at her and meowed.

Pressing a calming hand to her chest, Ronnie laughed shakily. She never figured Diego for a cat person.

"Hey there," she cooed. She scratched the kitty behind the ear, and it purred, eyes squinting into fine slits.

Ronnie cleaned up the spilled water and left the kitchen, walking quietly back down the hall. She cast another glance at the photos, turned out the light, and entered the bedroom.

She crawled into bed, and Diego wrapped his arms around her from behind.

"What's this?" he asked in a disgruntled voice. He tugged on the shirt.

"Your shirt."

He started pulling it off her body, and she lifted up so he could get it all the way off. He tossed it to the floor and closed his arms around her.

Ronnie nestled her bottom against his pelvis. "What's your cat's name?"

"Bonkers. This is her house. She just lets me stay here."

Ronnie giggled. "What kind of name is Bonkers?"

He took so long to answer, at first she thought he wouldn't.

"When she was a kitten, she had an inner ear infection that caused bouts of dizziness. She bumped into walls and couldn't jump for shit. We called her Bonkers before we realized she needed to see the vet. She's all better now, but the name stuck."

Ronnie played with the fine hairs on his forearm.

"We?"

Another pause. "Me and my ex-fiancée."

"You were engaged."

"Yes."

"I saw the photos." She paused a beat before asking the next question. "You have a daughter?"

The silence lasted even longer this time. His body became very still.

"I don't mean to pry, I—"

"Had. I had a daughter," he said, his voice sounding raw and pained.

Chapter Sixteen

Diego should have told Ronnie everything before, but this part of his past was not only painful, it opened him up to judgment when he fully explained how he responded to the trauma of losing his child.

He rolled away from Ronnie and stared up at the ceiling, bracing for the jagged pain that always materialized when he went back in time.

Ronnie stirred and turned onto her side to face him.

"My daughter's name was Matilda. She was three years old when she died," he whispered. Agony stomped all over his chest.

Ronnie placed a comforting hand on his arm. "I'm so sorry."

"The M in D&M Towing is for my daughter. To honor her memory in a small way."

"Diego, if you don't want to talk about this, you don't have to." Her voice vibrated with concern, but now that he'd started, he couldn't stop. He wanted to tell her everything—share every aspect of his life with her. The good and the bad.

"My father was a mean sonofabitch who regularly got drunk and beat my mother. When he tired of beating her, he turned his rage on me and my younger brother, Javier."

Bitterness shadowed his voice. The memories of living in constant fear of the man who should have been his protector and guide into adulthood lived on as a nasty reminder of the kind of man he should never become.

Ronnie kissed his shoulder. The touch of her soft lips further encouraged his confession.

"Matilda wasn't planned, but when Loisa, my girlfriend, became pregnant, I was excited. Right away, we moved in together and started saving money to get married and start a life together."

He welcomed the opportunity to have the joys he missed growing up. Stability. A normal family. Things other people took for granted.

"How did she die?" Ronnie asked quietly.

He took a breath. "She attended a kids' birthday party at a friend's house and drowned in the pool." He closed his eyes to stem the force of the pain that filled him at the thought of his little angel, so young, so innocent, dying like that. "Waking up every day was too hard, and every time I looked at Loisa, I blamed her."

"Why?" Ronnie asked.

He glanced at her. "Because I never wanted Matilda to go to the party in the first place. Not without one of us present. But I was at work, and Loisa let her cousin take Matilda to the party. Said it gave her a break to run errands...or something. I can't remember the explanation anymore." He ran a hand down his face. "I know it was an accident. I know it wasn't her fault, but I struggled to forgive her."

Wounded and hurt, he could hardly stand to look at the woman he'd once loved and planned to marry.

Ronnie touched his jaw, and the simple gesture encouraged him to continue talking.

"Bonkers was Matilda's kitten. She kept bugging me about a kitten. 'Papa, I want a kitty. Please, Papa.' She wore me down." He smiled.

With his father spending his paychecks on women and drinking, he'd missed out on so much growing up, and didn't want the same for his own daughter. He took extra shifts, worked overtime whenever he could, to make sure she and Loisa were well provided for.

He surprised Matilda one day when he came home from work. He hid the kitten in a cardboard box with a red bow around her neck, and presented the gift to his daughter when she rushed to meet him at the door. For several days they didn't have a name, but Matilda hugged and kissed her kitten at every opportunity. The two were inseparable.

"When my daughter died, I self-medicated— started drinking heavily." Diego laughed hollowly. "You'd think I'd know better, but I needed to numb the pain." He swallowed hard, and felt his features tightening. "I lost myself down a dark hole of self-pity and pain and regret. Wishing I—*we* could have done something different. My self-destructive behavior cost me friends and family. They couldn't tolerate being around me anymore. They lost their sympathy for me, and I sank deeper into depression. My relationship with Loisa tanked, obviously."

"That's why I never see you drink," Ronnie said.

"That's why you never see me drink," Diego confirmed with a nod. He searched her face for disappointment or disgust, but saw neither. Only a wrinkled brow and eyes filled with concern. "I'm an alcoholic, Veronica."

She didn't flinch or blink. "What prompted you to get sober?"

He heaved out a breath. "I was sitting in a jail cell, six weeks into a three-month sentence. Everyone had turned their backs on me. Not my cousin Tomas, though." He laughed softly, still not comprehending how or why Tomas stood by his side, believing in him, encouraging him. "I didn't hear from Loisa. I didn't hear from Javier. One day, Tomas asked me if I was satisfied. If this was all I wanted in life." He fell silent, going back in time to that day. "I thought about his question later when I was lying on my bunk. I realized that wasn't all I wanted in my life. I could do better. I was meant for better."

He tilted his head toward Ronnie. She watched him with rapt attention and nonjudgmental eyes.

"When I got out, I attended AA meetings and cleaned up my act. Tomas invited me to Atlanta to start over, said I could stay with him, but I didn't want to be a burden. Both of my parents were gone by then, so I sold their house, gave Javier his cut, and found a place of my own here."

He didn't spend much, and when the opportunity presented itself to buy the towing company, he jumped at the chance.

He turned onto his side and looked into Ronnie's eyes. "I don't drink anymore, but that doesn't mean it's been easy. I've been sober for three years and twenty-one days, and I don't see any reason why I have to go back down that path. But I should've told you from the beginning."

"Thank you for telling me everything, but I'm not worried. I'm pretty tough. And I'll hit you upside the head with my crescent wrench if you get any ideas about drinking again."

"Yes, ma'am." Diego chuckled and she grinned at him.

Ronnie traced a finger down his nose. "It's okay, you know. Everybody makes mistakes."

"That was a major one."

"But you overcame. Doesn't matter if you fall. As long as you get back up."

Chapter Seventeen

Every year Tomas threw a huge Memorial Day BBQ at his property in the country. He and his wife Talia owned a townhouse in a trendy neighborhood in Atlanta, but they spent most of their time in a sprawling ranch an hour outside of the city, and that was where Diego was headed. The huge property contained a private lake, and his cousin loved the fact that the nearest house was miles away.

Ronnie had said she couldn't make the trip out until later, so Diego arrived before the festivities started to offer his help, and thought he could also use the opportunity to ask his cousin for a favor.

He pulled up the dirt driveway and spotted Tomas, wearing a black apron and "Grillmaster" emblazoned in white on the front with a lightning bolt going through the word. He kept an eye on his almost three-year-old son Manuel, who was driving an F-150 yellow toy truck around the yard.

Wearing a red cap turned backward on his head

and big plastic sunglasses, the little boy grinned from ear to ear on the big toy. Manuel was a shade darker than his father, a miniature version of Tomas with the same whiskey-colored eyes, smile, and facial features.

Before climbing out of the truck cab, Diego lifted the dark brown fedora from the seat beside him and dropped it loosely on his head.

When Manuel saw Diego coming toward them, he waved. Diego grinned at the little boy and lifted a hand in greeting.

Tomas was a diehard charcoal user, and the aroma of cooking meat filled the air. Hamburgers and hotdogs worked on the kettle grill while meats cooked on the barrel grill.

"You're here early," Tomas said, taking his eyes off his son for a second.

"Couldn't wait to see you," Diego joked.

Tomas chuckled. "I seriously doubt that."

"Where's Talia?" Diego looked around the property, taking in the dogwood and scarlet oak trees, and the way the sun's rays sparkled on the lake's surface.

"Making sure the rest of the food arrives and finishing up the sides."

Hard to believe that his wife was handling any of the dishes. When the couple first started dating, Talia didn't know her way around the kitchen and Tomas did all the cooking. Now they shared the culinary duties.

Diego stood silently beside his cousin, watching the big black tires of Manuel's truck roll over the grass and the bare, rocky patches in the yard.

"What exactly does Talia do at the marketing firm?" Diego asked.

"She's the senior vice president of creative services. Why?"

Diego watched his cousin transfer charred hotdogs into an aluminum pan. "I have a favor I need to ask you," he said.

"Okay." Tomas added uncooked hotdogs to the grill.

"Do you think she'd do a small job for me?"

Tomas looked over his shoulder. "For you personally?"

"Actually, for Ronnie's mechanic shop, Taylor Automotive. She needs help."

Tomas lifted an eyebrow. "You want me to ask my wife, who handles multi-million dollar accounts, to do a marketing plan for your girlfriend?"

Girlfriend. He and Ronnie didn't use labels and the word sounded strange.

"She's not my girlfriend," Diego mumbled.

"You spend all your time with her."

"I care about her. Listen, I just want your help. Talia created a marketing plan for your business," Diego pointed out.

His cousin had left his job as the foreman of a construction company to start his own business remodeling homes, work he'd done on the side for years. After collecting market research, Talia created a plan that included designing stationery and matching business cards, and rolling out a media campaign that included a large billboard on Highway 85.

"I sleep next to her every night. I have some pull," Tomas said, with a sly smile.

"Help me out, Tomas."

His cousin cast thoughtful eyes in his direction. "You really like this woman, eh?'

Diego shrugged. "I want to help her."

Tomas's eyes followed his son. "*Mijo*," he called. "Come back this way," he said in Spanish.

Manuel reversed the truck and turned around, driving across the yard.

"What's the name of her shop again?" Tomas asked.

Diego relaxed. He thought he'd have to do more persuading, but Tomas had given in much easier than he'd expected. "Taylor Automotive & Repair. Right next to my place."

"I'll tell Talia, but no promises."

"Tell Talia what?"

The umber-skinned Talia, whose dignified appearance relayed the fact that she came from money, squeezed between them. It was funny to see them together, his cousin looking almost untamed with his long hair, T-shirt, and jeans. Meanwhile, Talia appeared chic and feminine in a maxi skirt and white shirt that dipped off her shoulder, and her long thick hair pulled up into a pile of curls on top of her head.

Tomas placed his arm around her and cupped the uncovered shoulder. "My cousin wants you to use your considerable talent to help him capture the undying love of a particular female." He kissed her temple.

"Oh really?" Talia raised a neat brow. "Sounds serious."

Diego glared at his cousin.

Tomas's mouth twitched at the corners. "I think it is," he said in a stage whisper.

"How are you feeling, *prima*?" Diego asked.

"Look at him, changing the subject," Talia said.

"We see right through you."

Diego shrugged. "You're pregnant, and I want to know how you and the baby are doing."

She smiled contentedly. "We're fine."

Tomas rubbed his wife's shoulder, and she leaned into him. Talia was ten weeks pregnant—too early to tell the sex of the baby.

"And of course I'll help you," Talia added. "I can do a quick market analysis, but I'll have to work on that project in between my obligations at the agency."

"No problem. By the way, it's a surprise for her, so the information you have access to will be limited to what I can provide."

Talia's eyebrows came together. "That's going to make it difficult to come up with a good plan."

"It doesn't have to be too in-depth."

"You're sure?"

"Positive."

"Okay, if you say so."

Diego slapped his hands together. "Okay, what do you need me to do before the guests start arriving?"

"To start, you can help me set up the tables and chairs." Tomas turned to his wife. "*Querida*, you should take Manuel inside. We'll have a hard time keeping an eye on him while we're working out here. Manuel, come back and go inside with Mommy."

Manuel glanced over his shoulder but kept moving.

"*Ven aca, mijo*," Tomas called.

The little boy shook his head, vehemently. "No, Daddy."

"*Manuel, ven aca ahora*," Tomas said, tone harder.

Manuel ignored the stern command, and Tomas uttered a curse in Spanish and took off after the toddler. The little boy continued driving, looking over his shoulder as if he could outrun his father in the toy truck, which couldn't be going more than three or four miles per hour.

Talia's hand touched Diego's arm. "The Anniversary is coming up. You doing okay?" she asked, concern in her eyes. Like Tomas, she was older, and looked out for Diego.

She'd asked the question because the time of year he dreaded the most was soon upon him. Last year he'd almost slipped back into depression, the Anniversary coming on the heels of the stress of starting a new business. She and Tomas encouraged him to take a couple of days off, and they let him stay out here, where the fresh air and quiet soothed his tormented thoughts.

"I'm good," he answered, swallowing past the tightness in his throat.

She patted his arm. "You know we're here if you need us."

He looked away in time to see Tomas grab the back of the truck. Manuel let out a high-pitched scream and Tomas scooped up the little boy from the seat. He then proceeded to march across the yard with a wailing, kicking Manuel tucked under his arm like a football, dragging the big yellow truck behind him.

Talia took the little boy from his father and he clung to her, sobbing pitifully into her breasts. Diego picked up the giant sunglasses that had fallen off his face, while Tomas carried the truck onto the porch.

"Shh. Stop now." Talia rubbed her son's back.

"I'll flip this meat and then we'll get to work," Tomas said, walking over to the grills.

Talia continued to talk in a soothing voice to their

son. She took the sunglasses from Diego. "Why didn't you listen to Daddy, hmm? He told you to come back. You have to listen to Daddy, okay?" She walked up the steps.

The sight of Talia lovingly cradling his little cousin gutted him. How many times had he held his little girl in his arms, cradling her in much the same way to soothe her tears when she skinned a knee or crawled into bed with him and Loisa because she was certain there was a monster in the closet?

Because of the violence and chaos of his upbringing, as a young man he'd welcomed the chance to have a stable home environment. Matilda and Loisa offered everything he missed out on. Then it was all yanked away.

He loved Tomas and Talia. They were his family. But sometimes, the display of their happiness was a painful reminder of the emptiness in his own life. Not only what was missing, but what he had lost.

Chapter Eighteen

Ronnie drove with one hand along the two-lane road with the window down and her elbow propped on the door, letting the wind whoosh through the cabin of the truck. The cool air whipped over her skin and counteracted the warmth of the sun. She inhaled deeply, appreciating the cleaner, fresher smell of her surroundings.

Zooming by a sign advertising strawberry picking, she smiled. She had fond childhood memories of she and her cousins excitedly filling plastic containers of strawberries, and at the end of the trip sitting in the back of her father's truck with their prizes on their laps, gorging on the sweet fruit on their way home. Her aunt complained about the amount of berries, but whipped up all sorts of treats from the bounty— strawberry pie, strawberry shortcake, strawberry jam, and Ronnie's personal favorite, chocolate-covered strawberries.

A large white truck lumbered by, laden with crates

of vegetables and Tottle Farms painted on the door. The driver honked twice and waved, and Ronnie waved back. Although she didn't want to move out of metro Atlanta, she understood the appeal of living so far outside the city limits.

Arriving at her destination, she turned onto the dirt road. Numerous vehicles lined either side of the lane, too many to count.

"Whoa," Ronnie murmured, parking behind a Jeep.

Latin music played loud and strong when Ronnie approached the house. Thanks to Diego, she'd gained an appreciation for the genre. He had educated her about different forms: bachata, merengue, salsa, reggaeton—but those were only a few.

He was very loyal to a Cuban hip-hop/Afropunk musician by the name of X Alfonso. Whenever they rode in his truck, more than likely the musician's husky vocals could be heard blasting through the speakers. But she recognized the current thumping beat as the extremely popular "Danza Kuduro" by Don Omar. She didn't understand the words, but every time Diego played the hit, she tapped her feet in time to the upbeat tempo.

Continuing to walk, she scanned the property for Diego. Kids ran around screaming and laughing, and she pulled up short when a little boy careened toward her, screeching with a little girl hot on his heels.

"Excuse me!" he cried, dodging Ronnie.

They both ran toward the tire swing, where two teenaged boys observed the kids playing near the lake.

She'd texted Diego when she neared the property, but didn't see him anywhere among the group—a mixture of all ages and races, eating and drinking together, some even dancing under the shade of one of the many flowering dogwood trees dotting the grounds.

"Ronnie, is that you?" a surprised male voice said.

A little over six feet, with a wiry build and chocolate skin, Edgar stood a few feet away, eyes wide and mouth hanging open. Small world.

"Hi. What—"

She broke off when he rushed over and pulled her into a tight hug. A couple of seconds passed before Ronnie remembered to hug him back.

"What are you doing here?" she asked when he released her. "Do you know Tomas and Talia?"

"No, a friend invited me. You?"

"No, I...Tomas's cousin invited me, Diego." This was the hard part, explaining her relationship with Diego. They were a couple, but not really. They slept together, but she wasn't sure she could actually call him her boyfriend, and he seemed perfectly fine with the current situation. She, on the other hand, hated the uncertainty.

He frowned. "I don't think I met him. But you look great!" he exclaimed, standing back and examining her. His gaze ran over the cutoff denim shorts and purple tank top.

"Thank you." Her cheeks burned impossibly hot at the unexpected compliment.

"I feel terrible about the night we met. I can't believe you worked on my car in the parking lot." He shook his head. "I was too embarrassed to call and follow up." His eyes dipped to her legs again.

Ronnie shifted from one foot to the other. He was obviously checking her out, and while she was flattered, the attention did surprise her. During their initial meeting, she never got the impression that he was very interested. Perhaps the shirt-dress didn't impress him much, but he clearly liked the shorts.

"Don't worry about it."

"So…are you seeing anyone?" he asked tentatively.

"Um…" Again, she didn't quite know what to say. "Sort of. The guy I mentioned, Diego."

His mouth downturned. "Guess I missed my shot, huh?"

"I…um…"

Edgar smiled. "Don't answer. Come on, let's see if we can find Diego." He placed a hand between her shoulder blades, and she tried not to read too much into the fact that he was touching her yet again.

As they walked side by side, Ronnie searched the grounds. Her eyes bounced from person to person until she spotted Diego during another glance at the porch "I see him now."

Edgar followed her line of vision. "Where?"

She pointed. "In the green T-shirt."

"Oh."

She understood the subdued response. Diego looked particularly scrumptious in a green, fitted T-shirt with white letters and jeans that fit snugly but not tightly over his lean hips. He looked downright potent and dripping with confidence. Two woven bracelets, one made of leather and the other of yarn, circled his right wrist, and a chocolate fedora rested in a casual position on the back of his head.

He bounced his head to "Danza Kuduro," smiling as he talked. He had a two-day growth of hair on his face because he'd become lazy over the long weekend and refused to shave. Not that she minded. She quite enjoyed the sweet burn of facial hair against her inner thigh when they made love.

He finally saw her and she waved at him and smiled.

"Now that you've found your guy, I'll leave you alone," Edgar said. Regret in his eyes, he squeezed her arm, his hand lingering a little too long by dragging across her skin, before he walked away.

When Ronnie looked at the porch again, Diego's eyes followed Edgar's progress across the yard, a smile no longer on his face. Ronnie approached the stairs and right away recognized the two men with Diego as the ones at Dilligan's the night he beat her in pool.

Based on an earlier conversation, she guessed the tallest one was Tomas. He had an arm wrapped around a petite, dark-skinned woman standing in front of him, who moved her hips ever so slightly to the music. She must be Talia.

A wide grin spread across Diego's face, and he nudged Tomas. All eyes turned to Ronnie as she ascended the stairs.

"You finally made it. I was beginning to worry," Diego said, slipping an arm around her waist and pulling her close to his side.

"I texted you."

Frowning, he took out the phone and saw the text. "My little cousin Manuel was playing with the phone earlier. I didn't receive an alert. He must have changed the settings."

Diego tugged a loose string on her jeans. "These are short," he said in a low voice, so no one else could hear.

Heat suffused her cheeks. "I cut off an old pair of jeans. Anika showed me how to make them distressed using sandpaper."

Her happiness changed to bewilderment when she noted the hard set to his jaw. The comment wasn't so much a compliment as an observation.

He made the introductions, introducing Ryan, Talia, and Tomas, and introducing her as Veronica.

"But you can call me Ronnie," she added.

While they spoke, Ryan's wife, Shawna, a woman with russet skin and her long hair in a neat ponytail, came from inside the house with a chubby baby boy in her arms.

"How old is he?" Ronnie asked. She touched his hand, and his little fist closed around her finger. She wagged her hand and the boy rewarded her with a bright smile.

"Eight months." Shawna beamed.

"He's adorable," Ronnie cooed.

"Are you hungry?" Talia asked.

Ronnie dragged her attention away from the baby. "I could definitely eat." She'd barely eaten all day, saving her appetite after Diego told her about all the food Tomas and Talia prepared and bought for the annual event.

"There are hotdogs, burgers, chicken—plenty to eat," Diego said.

Talia pointed at Ryan and Diego. "You two need to help Tomas bring out more chairs and move the picnic tables under the trees."

"And bring out more ice and drinks," Shawna added.

"So you need the men to handle the heavy lifting?" Ryan asked, flexing his muscles.

Shawna giggled and shoved her husband. "Just go. We'll take care of Ronnie."

"You don't have to babysit me. Just point me in the right direction and I can fix my own plate."

There was plenty of food outside, but Ronnie followed Ryan and Diego into the house where there was more food and she could wash her hands. They passed a living room filled with large, traditional furniture in dark hues. Ten men crowded around the television watching a White Sox and Cleveland Indians baseball game and yelling at the screen.

The large eat-in kitchen contained high-end Viking appliances, and it was obvious the hosts replenished the food outside from in here, where covered dishes lined almost every surface. Diego and Ryan left with the additional drinks and ice, and Ronnie reviewed her choices from the mouth-watering spread. She placed an extra char-grilled hotdog on the plate and added ribs, potato salad, and baked beans.

"This should get me started," she said to herself. She grabbed a cold beer and made her way toward the front, but loud cheering made her pause in the doorway of the living room.

Through instant replay, she saw one of the players slide into home plate.

Ronnie eased into the room. Diego was busy, so she could hang out for a minute and eat and watch the game.

She walked over to the leather sofa where a heavyset black male sat sipping a beer. "Mind if I sit?"

"Not at all. Have a seat."

"What's the score?" she asked, settling down.

"Four to two, in favor of the Indians," came the reply.

"I see you got the same idea I did," a familiar voice said to her right.

Ronnie looked up to see Edgar standing beside the couch.

"Mind if I join you?"

"There's plenty of room." She and the other man scooted over and Edgar joined them.

Ronnie bit into a rib and settled down to watch the game.

Chapter Nineteen

Almost an hour later, Diego went in search of Ronnie. Helping Tomas straighten up around the property kept him busy for some time. Then one of the guests tried to leave while intoxicated. His wife came running and begged Tomas and Diego to intervene. After extensive talking didn't work, they wrestled him to the ground and took away the keys.

Diego thought Ronnie was in good hands with the other women, but neither Talia nor Shawna had seen her, and he felt a twinge of guilt for leaving her alone for so long.

Except she wasn't alone. He found her in the living room, the only female among the men. Right at home between two black guys on the leather couch. The wiry one rested an arm along the back of the chair, behind her head. Earlier, when he saw the same guy with Ronnie, something in his face, his demeanor, suggested a more than friendly interest.

An unnatural feeling crawled up the back of

Diego's neck to his scalp. Ronnie spent a lot of time in the company of the opposite sex. At Taylor Automotive. At the sports bar. But seeing her here, surrounded by all these men, struck a nerve. To date, the only woman he'd ever heard her talk about was her cousin, Anika.

Doesn't she know any women?

The crawling sensation tightened his shoulders.

The room erupted, the men hollering at the TV screen when a ball player was pronounced safe on a run. Ronnie leaped from the chair, lifted a hand in the air, and crowed victoriously.

"Did you see that?" she yelled in the face of the man to her left.

She didn't see Diego at the door, nor did she notice how the gaze of the man to her right lingered on her ass in his face.

Diego gritted his teeth. Those shorts were too damn short. One more inch and he'd see the underside of her bottom.

Her admirer jumped to his feet and yelled, "Yes!" Then he grabbed Ronnie around the waist and lifted her off the floor.

Diego saw red. He marched into the room, and by then the man had put Ronnie down, but his hand remained on her shoulder as they watched the instant replay, as if he couldn't resist touching her. Tension tightened in Diego's shoulders as the irritation turned into full-on pain and he faced the other man.

"*¿Qué pasa, pendejo?*" Possessive anger coursed through his veins. Not only had this man been ogling her, he'd put his damn hands on her, and Diego didn't doubt for a minute the guy knew he and Ronnie were together.

Her admirer dropped his hand from her shoulder, and the smile vanished from Ronnie's face. They may not know that he called the man an asshole, but the hostility in his face made his displeasure clear.

"Diego, hi," Ronnie said in an overly cheery voice. "This is Edgar. Edgar, this is Diego."

"Nice to meet you," Edgar said.

Neither man extended a hand.

"You should keep your hands to yourself, Edgar," Diego said, steel in his voice.

Ronnie's eyes widened. "Diego." She laughed shakily, clearly embarrassed.

Edgar lifted his hands in surrender. "I understand."

"Do you?"

Edgar swallowed. "I got a little carried away."

The room had fallen into an awkward silence, the only sound the announcers covering the baseball game. Diego flexed the fingers of his hand.

"Can we go, please?" Ronnie asked, gaze jerking around the room at their audience.

Diego didn't move.

"Diego, please."

His gaze shot to her, and her pleading expression finally got through to him. He took her by the wrist and pulled her out of the room and down the hall, into the kitchen where they could talk alone.

She yanked her arm away and whirled on him right away. "What the hell!"

"Is that what you've been doing for the past hour?" He was being an asshole but couldn't stop himself. He clenched and unclenched his hands, itching to smash something.

"I was watching the game. I only planned to sit

down for a few minutes while you worked. I lost track of time." A perfectly reasonable response that did nothing to assuage his anger.

"Do you really think it's a good idea for you to sit between all these men, dressed like that?" he asked in a vicious whisper.

Her wide eyes stretched wider. "Dressed like..." Ronnie glanced down at her clothes. "What's wrong with the way I'm dressed?"

"The shorts. The tank top. Come on."

Technically, there was nothing wrong with her clothes. Half the women at the picnic wore some variation of the same outfit, but what bothered him were the subtle changes he saw.

She used to wear loose-fitting clothes and didn't care much about her appearance. Now she wore booty shorts and a shirt that showed off her toned arms and was so tight on her breasts he damn near saw the capillaries in her nipples.

"The way I dress bothers you? This?"

"Whose attention are you trying to get?" Diego demanded.

He didn't get jealous. Ever. After Loisa cheated, he adopted a new perspective on relationships. If a woman wanted to step out on him while they were in a committed relationship, he'd show her the door. Why waste time with someone who didn't want to be with him and him alone?

So he couldn't comprehend the irrational monster that reared its hideous head where Ronnie was concerned. Why did it bother him so much that within the past week she'd started smelling different? She continued to use vanilla in her hair, but no more hibiscus-scented soap. A light, flowery fragrance perfumed her skin. And she put her slender figure on display more and more, in revealing clothes that at first he thought she only wore for him, but now he questioned if she was interested in snagging the attention of men like Edgar, who obviously had the hots for her.

Ronnie placed her hands on her hips. "I can't believe you asked me whose attention I'm trying to get. But since you did, I'm not trying to get anyone's attention."

"No?" Diego edged nearer. Watching her closely. "Tell the truth. You don't get a little thrill from having men check you out? From knowing that Edgar and at least half the men in there like looking at your pretty legs? Your perfect breasts?"

He was getting hard just thinking about her body in those terms.

She blinked and swallowed. "Everyone likes to be noticed by the opposite sex. It's only natural."

"So you admit it."

"I'm not admitting anything." She heaved a loud sigh. "Look, I'm not used to this type of reaction."

"Well, get used to it," Diego snarled. "I'm not going to sit still and let another man put his fucking hands all over my woman. He's lucky I didn't punch him in his goddamn face with that slick-ass move."

Her eyes widened. "Lower your voice."

"I will not lower my *fucking* voice!"

A lanky teenaged boy pulled up short at the entrance to the kitchen. "Um…Talia sent me in here to get a tray of chicken."

"Over there." Diego jabbed a finger at the containers sitting on the stove.

The young man rushed over and lifted the

aluminum foil on the first container, confirming that it was the chicken. He then picked up the meat and hurried out.

Diego paced the floor, dragging large quantities of air into his lungs with deep, heavy inhalations. His insides burned with jealous anger.

Ronnie stood in front of the window, resting her back against the sink and staring at the floor. "So I'm your woman?"

Diego stopped moving at the quietly asked question.

She lifted her gaze to him, the question repeated in her eyes.

He ambled over to stand directly in front of her. "Yes, you're my woman." It was time he made that clear. No more ambiguity.

"If I'm your woman, you should trust me."

"I trust you. It's them I don't trust." He pointed at the door.

"No one is paying attention to me like you think they are."

"You simply don't notice."

It was laughable, really, her lack of guile when it came to men. Even women noticed her. Shawna had commented on her toned body and "fierce" haircut.

What she mistook for lack of attention from men was actually intimidation. They'd learned she'd cut them down with harsh words or a well-placed glare, and while he teased her about her "resting bitch face," the expression kept most men from approaching.

She might not be the kind of woman who stopped traffic, but in a room full of men, unless they were all blind, she definitely did not go unnoticed. Especially with her beautiful brown legs on display and a tank top that hugged her torso so well it showed off her pert breasts and left nothing to the imagination.

Diego placed a hand on either side of her and gazed into her eyes. He could get lost in those warm brown pools. "What if I tell you I'm jealous?" he asked. His gut clenched. He felt vulnerable, baring his soul.

"I would say you have nothing to be jealous about," Ronnie replied, her voice whisper soft. "I'd be a liar if I said I wasn't flattered when another man pays attention to me, but I only want your attention. I only care about what you think." She lifted the hat off his head and placed it on hers at a jaunty angle. "You always talk about how nice my legs are. I wore these shorts for you."

Diego grimaced. Maybe he was an asshole.

"Do you trust me?" Ronnie sifted her fingers through his hair. The light touch further calmed his raging temper.

He rested his forehead against hers. His failed relationship with Loisa affected him more than he realized. The changes he saw in Ronnie were signs he ignored in his ex during his periods of insobriety. Only later did he recognize that the shift in her behavior had been caused by another man.

A man who bought her lace panties, perfume, and jewelry. Which she proudly wore with confidence. Right under Diego's nose. And he never had a clue.

"I trust you," he said, throat tight.

"Good."

He looked deeply into her eyes and saw nothing but sweetness and affection.

"*But* you're still coming outside with me. You're not going back into that room."

"Diego."

He touched his mouth to hers. Gently, softly, he kissed her, swirling his tongue between her lips. One hand moved under her shirt and found soft skin. He grasped her waist and pulled her closer. Nudging her mouth wider, he casually swept from one end to the next, tasting the sweet-as-honey flavor.

"Let's go before I take you right here in my cousin's kitchen." She giggled softly and he took her by the hand. "Am I going to get my hat back?"

She pressed the fedora flatter on her head. "Nope. It's mine for the rest of the evening. That's your punishment for making me miss the rest of the game."

They joined the festivities outside, and as darkness fell, he watched her playing with the children and joking around with his friends and family.

He'd learn to accept the camaraderie she shared with men another day. He knew that without a doubt. Those relationships were part of who she was, and in all honesty he didn't want her to change. But right now, he wanted to keep her close. Because as much as she fit in comfortably with the men, there was no denying that Ronnie Taylor was all woman.

Chapter Twenty

Ronnie couldn't believe it. Her father was finally taking Miss Loretta on a date. Ever since the neighbor escorted him to the doctor for his cataract surgery, the two had become very close. They went to church together and even carpooled to the grocery store on Saturdays.

Nervous but excited, Ronnie bounced anxiously in the entryway, waiting for her father to descend the stairs. Miss Loretta liked him well enough, but he could be rather abrasive, and she wanted to inspect his clothing and give him a few pointers before he left.

Ezekiel finally came down the stairs in a light blue shirt and colorful tie, over which he wore a dark jacket and dark slacks. He looked very dashing.

When his feet hit the hardwood floor, Ezekiel smoothed a hand down his tie. "How do I look?"

Ronnie made a big show of doing a full inspection. She circled him and checked out the shiny shoes and his newly cut hair.

"Not bad," she said, placing her hands on her hips.

"You think I don't know how to impress a lady?"

"Clearly you do." She smiled fondly at him. "Enjoy yourself, okay?"

"I plan to."

"And be nice."

"I know how to be nice, nugget."

His eyes were focused on a point on the wall behind her, and he continued to smooth a hand down his tie. He was so deep in thought, she was certain he didn't even know he was doing it.

"I need a new bathrobe," he said, his voice quivering a little.

Her chest tightened. This was a big step for her father. "Okay."

His eyes focused on her face. "We can put the old one in a box. I don't want to throw it away. We should put it in storage or something."

Ronnie nodded. "That's a good idea."

Ezekiel's hand dropped to his side.

Ronnie kissed his cheek, leaving her mouth pressed to his skin for a long time. "It's okay, Daddy."

"Yeah."

The dinner date was at five, so it was still light out, and she stood in the doorway and watched him get in the car. "Call me if you're going to stay out all night so I don't worry," she said.

Her father glared at her out the window, and Ronnie laughed so hard her stomach hurt. Ezekiel pulled into Miss Loretta's driveway and walked to the front door. He rang the bell and waited.

Miss Loretta came out in a curly red wig—fuller

and thicker than the others Ronnie had seen her wear before.

"Go ahead, Miss Loretta," she murmured.

Her father took the neighbor by the arm and escorted her to the car. After she was seated, he walked around to the driver's side and paused. He lifted a hand at Ronnie, and she waved.

So many years had passed since her father dated, and for that brief moment, she felt like a parent seeing her child off to the prom or their first date.

Seconds later, they pulled away.

****

One Friday evening, rather than go out, Ronnie and Diego stayed at his place binge-watching episodes of *Battle Creek*, a show starring Josh Duhamel that should never have been cancelled, as far as Ronnie was concerned.

Two half-eaten extra-large boxes of pizza lay open on the coffee table, and Ronnie had a leg draped over Diego's thigh. Bonkers lounged atop the armrest of the sofa, eyes closed, purring contentedly at Diego's continuous petting and ear scratches. He'd once explained to Ronnie that Bonkers possessed a mean streak. If he didn't shower her with attention when she demanded it, she shredded the toilet tissue in the bathroom.

Ronnie wore a pair of drawstring shorts under one of Diego's white sleeveless undershirts that she'd grown quite fond of for their roominess and scent of him.

He flung his arm around her shoulder and she snuggled closer.

"How did the date with Miss Loretta go?" he asked.

"Excellent. Daddy and Miss Loretta spend even more time together now, and they're planning a senior trip with the church. Outside of the volunteer work he does, I've never seen him so active."

"I'm a little jealous," Diego said darkly.

Ronnie giggled. "Your bromance is going to have to cool down for a while. I was starting to feel a little insecure, that maybe you only came to the house to see him and not me."

Diego and her father had become close. On Sundays, the three watched sports and Ezekiel taught Diego how to grill, going so far as to share the recipe for his secret rub.

"Unless she plans to work with him in the yard, I don't have anything to worry about," Diego said.

He helped Ezekiel work in the yard and did odd jobs around the house. Diego loved to garden, having a small vegetable and herb garden that produced hearty tomatoes. He helped Ezekiel with his own garden, and in the front of the house, they'd planted flowers. The S-shaped design Diego created rivaled their professor-neighbor's flowerbeds. Both Diego and Ezekiel spent a lot of time in the yard, pruning bushes and cutting back hedges—work Ronnie had no desire to do.

On more than one occasion she'd found the duo sitting on the back patio, Diego with his chair tipped back and both of them sipping lemonade or iced tea. They discussed politics, music, women, and any topic that came to mind. Two men just enjoying each other's company. During those moments, she left them alone so they could have the time to themselves.

She recognized the situation for what it was. Ezekiel had become a father figure. An older male

Diego could look up to and spend time with—an experience missing from his childhood.

"Have you decided if you'll attend Daddy's dinner party?"

Sumpter Technical College had arranged a special dinner for Ezekiel, a thank you for the hours he'd spent giving the students a real-world view of being a mechanic. His no-nonsense straight talk, as well as the wealth of knowledge he provided, was well received not only by the students, but by the teachers. The dinner happened to be the same night as the Anniversary, the day Diego's daughter passed away.

"I think it'll be good for you to do something, instead of staying home by yourself," Ronnie said lightly.

She didn't want to push too hard. Normally he spent the Anniversary alone, but she'd suggested the night out could help keep his mind off the tragedy of losing his daughter.

"I've been thinking about what you said."

"And...?"

He looked at her. "You're right. There's absolutely no reason why I should stay home by myself. And it's nice what they're doing for your father."

"Are you sure?"

Diego nodded slowly, thoughtfully. "I don't think the pain will ever go away, but I don't want to stay in that place anymore. I want to move past it, and participating in normal activities is a good way to do that."

People grieved differently, and Diego had spent two years consumed with grief after his daughter died. To see him taking a step toward acceptance, without guilt or regret, warmed her heart.

Two episodes of *Battle Creek* later, Ronnie yawned and stretched. "I'm hungry again and I don't want any more pizza. Let's go out to eat. I want something hearty. You feel like steak?"

"Let me answer you this way—do Cubans do it better?"

"Well, I really don't know—" Her tart reply ended on a squeal when he snatched her onto his lap and held her tight so he could tickle her relentlessly. She hated the fact that she was ticklish, and he mercilessly punished her whenever he thought she was acting up.

"Stop! Stop!" Ronnie gasped. She wound up face down in the sofa with her hands behind her back and Diego's fingers poking her waistline.

"Do Cubans do it better?" he asked behind her.

"Yes! The best," she choked out, gasping and laughing at the same time.

He let her go and pulled her onto his lap. Ronnie pouted, swiping tears from her eyes. He just gave her one of his wicked smiles and nuzzled her neck. As usual, delicious tingles sprinkled along her neck and shoulders, making her small breasts feel heavy and full.

Goodness, this man drove her crazy. He cupped the back of her head and nipped at her jaw with his teeth and lips.

"I hate you so much," she said, angling her neck so he could drop more kisses with ease.

"But I *love* you," he whispered.

He'd said the words lightly, but they both stopped moving. There was nothing light about using that word. It may very well be the most powerful word in the world—in the universe. A word that at the same time it threatened weakness, offered strength. Broke hearts and mended them.

"Where do you want to go eat?" he asked, as though he hadn't dropped a bomb in the middle of their conversation.

"There's a Longhorn nearby," Ronnie responded with a saucy smile, following suit.

"Sounds good to me."

She wiggled from his lap. "Let me run to the bathroom and then we can leave."

Halfway to the bathroom, she doubled back and leaned over the back of the sofa and dropped a soft kiss to Diego's cheek. He looked up in surprise.

"I love you, too," she said, and scurried off. But not before she saw the way his green eyes lit up.

Chapter Twenty-one

Diego straightened the blue tie on his three-piece suit. In a few minutes, he needed to leave to meet Ronnie and her father for dinner at Hearty Kitchen, the restaurant the college booked to celebrate Ezekiel and his contributions.

As he checked his appearance for the last time in the mirror, the doorbell rang.

Frowning because he wasn't expecting anyone, Diego went to the door and inhaled a breath of shock when he saw Loisa standing there. Or rather a fragment of Loisa, because she clearly wasn't herself. She tottered on the black heels and braced both hands against the doorjamb. Looking up at him with both eyes almost closed, so that it was nigh on impossible that she could even see him, she said, "*Hola*, Diego." The words came out slurred.

Mierda. She was drunk.

A taxi backed out of his driveway and Loisa pushed past him, stumbling into the house and collapsing into a sprawl on the sofa.

He shut the door. She shouldn't be here. They'd had a long talk and he explained the situation—that he was in a committed relationship and she couldn't come and stay with him while she looked for an apartment.

He ran a hand over the back of his head, thinking hard about how to handle the situation. Dinner with Ronnie and Ezekiel now seemed like an impossibility.

"I know, I know. I shouldn't be here. You told me not to come, but I couldn't let you be alone tonight. It's the Anniversary. I had to come."

Diego walked over to the sofa and looked down at her. Bonkers, catnapping in the corner on her pillow, purred with one eye open, as if Loisa had disturbed her sleep.

"I wasn't going to be alone. I had plans."

"With who?" She sobered a little, sitting up with a wrinkled brow, hurt in her eyes.

"The woman I told you about." Not that he needed to explain anything to her.

"Does she know how important tonight is?" Loisa asked.

"Yes, and that's why I planned to spend the evening with her."

"You said you always spend the Anniversary alone." Accusation filled her voice, and she pouted.

Diego dropped to his haunches. She looked like a mess. Her clothes were in disarray, and a red stain colored the white blouse she wore half tucked into her skirt.

She was hurting, and she'd come to the one person she knew would understand the pain. Even though he hadn't planned on spending any time with her tonight, he couldn't turn her away. Certainly not in the state she was in.

"I normally do, but we can spend the Anniversary together tonight. If you want."

"I do want," she said, breathing the pungent scent of liquor into his face. "And you know what else I want?"

She bit her bottom lip, and Diego hesitated to respond. The look in Loisa's eyes unnerved him.

"I want another baby, Diego. I want another baby—maybe a boy this time. Don't you want another baby?" She released the top button of her blouse.

He held her hand to stop her from undressing. "Loisa, you're drunk. You don't know what you're doing."

"I do know what I'm doing." She leaned closer, trying to be seductive, and almost fell over onto him. He clutched her shoulders and settled her back onto the sofa. She closed her eyes, face wrinkled into a grimace. "I want a baby," she whispered. "I messed up. I want to make it up to you." A tear rolled down her cheek, and seeing her in such distress twisted his insides.

This was the woman he'd loved. The woman he thought he'd spend the rest of his life with, and she was still suffering and torturing herself over an event neither of them could have foreseen or prevented.

"It was an accident. I don't blame you," he said quietly. He couldn't argue that he'd blamed her at one time, but no more.

She opened eyes heavy with tears. "You left me. You stopped loving me because of what I did."

"I don't blame you anymore," Diego said quietly.

"Do you forgive me?" She grabbed his shoulders and fell into him, knocking them both to the ground. He lay on the floor with her on top of him, her quiet sobs tearing into his conscience.

"I forgave you a long time ago." He cupped the back of her head and stroked her hair. "Now you have to forgive yourself."

She sniffled. "I'm sorry I cheated. You needed me."

Diego stared up at the ceiling. "You needed me, too, and I wasn't there. We both screwed up, Loisa."

"Maybe we could start over." She lifted her head, dark streaks on her cheeks where her eye makeup mixed with the tears. Her eyes pleaded with him for another chance, but he couldn't lie or give her false hope.

"It's too late."

Her bottom lip quivered. "Don't you want another baby? Let me do that for you, Diego."

Diego brushed the tears from her cheeks with his thumbs. "Not right now."

She shook from the force of her tears. Fresh streaks replaced the ones he'd just removed. "I wish..." She dropped her head to his chest. "I never loved him, you know. I was just..."

"I know."

He rubbed her back. She had needed Diego, and he hadn't been available—physically or mentally. He was as much to blame for the dissolution of their relationship as she. He'd sought comfort in a bottle. She'd sought comfort in the arms of another man.

Diego lifted off the floor with her in his arms and took her into his bedroom. He gently placed her on the bed and removed her shoes. He covered her, and when he moved to leave the room, she lifted a hand toward him.

"You're not leaving me, are you?" she asked, in a pitifully feeble voice.

"I have to make a phone call. I'll be right back."

Diego closed the door quietly behind him and went back into the living room. Glancing over his shoulder to make sure Loisa didn't follow, he paced for a few minutes, thinking. Finally, he dialed Ronnie's number.

He hated to bail on her with such short notice, but he couldn't leave Loisa alone in this state.

Ronnie answered on the third ring. "Hi, I'm so glad you called. Daddy's running late, being a diva or something. I have no idea what's going on. We'll be late getting to the restaurant."

"Actually, that's why I called." Diego ran a hand through his hair. "I won't be able to make the dinner after all."

"What? Why not?"

He paused, debating whether or not to tell her about Loisa. "Something's come up. Something I need to handle." His relationship with her was strong, but even he knew it was a bad idea to tell your current girlfriend that your ex was sleeping in your bed. No matter how he tried to spin the story, it would sound bad, and he didn't want to disrupt Ronnie's good mood right before her father's event.

"Can I help?" Ronnie asked.

He heard the concern in her voice but didn't want her to worry. "I'm fine. This is just something I need to handle, something that's come up unexpectedly. But I'll call you tomorrow and you can tell me all about tonight."

"Well...if you're sure."

"Yes. I—"

He heard the bedroom door open, and when he turned around, Loisa stood looking at him. Her face was dry, but she'd let down her hair and, most disturbing of all, removed her skirt and blouse. She stood half-naked in his apartment, and he was fairly certain if he didn't move quickly, she'd be completely naked in a matter of seconds.

"I'll explain everything tomorrow, okay?"

"Oh. Okay, well have a good—"

Diego quickly hung up.

"Loisa, what are you doing?"

"I threw up on my clothes and don't have anything else to wear."

"I'll give you something to put on." He stood still, almost afraid to move because a part of him worried she'd pounce the minute he made any movement.

"One last time, Diego? Before you cut me off completely. Because I know it's coming." She appeared to have sobered a little while lying back there alone. Maybe throwing up helped.

"That's not going to happen."

She reached behind her and unhooked her bra. It fell to her feet. "Are you sure?"

Diego closed his eyes and bolstered his courage. It was going to be a long night.

Chapter Twenty-two

"Ezekiel Taylor, hurry up or I'm leaving without you!" Ronnie yelled up the stairs.

"You can't leave without me. I'm the guest of honor!" her father hollered back.

The strange cancellation conversation she'd just had with Diego gnawed at Ronnie. She understood why Miss Loretta couldn't make the event. She was out of town. But Diego's explanation didn't make sense.

Something's come up. What did that even mean? They spent so much time together that she'd developed a good sense of his moods, and something was definitely off. He didn't sound like himself at all, and he'd basically hung up on her, anxious to get off the phone.

She chewed on her bottom lip. She couldn't worry about that right now. The dinner with her father took precedence, and she'd check on Diego later.

Her father finally descended the stairs in a tan suit

and striped tie.

"Glad you could join me," Ronnie said.

"Do I look okay?" he asked. He stood in front of her and tugged on his suit sleeves.

"You look fine. Now let's go. By the way, Diego called and cancelled, so it's just you and me tonight."

"Well, that's how it's been all these years. Did he say why?"

"No, but I wouldn't be surprised if it's because of the Anniversary." Ronnie led the way to the kitchen. "He's probably not in the best of moods—maybe decided he didn't want to go out after all." She set the alarm and they both went into the garage.

"Maybe you should check on him after dinner," her father said, getting into the passenger seat of his car.

"I might do that." Ronnie climbed in and pressed the opener. The garage door lifted up. They pulled out and were on their way.

Sumpter Technical College had allowed Ezekiel to pick the restaurant where he'd like to eat, and he chose the newly opened Hearty Kitchen in Midtown. He and Ronnie knew the owners of the establishment, an old two-story house with a wraparound porch converted into the perfect location to serve American cuisine, featuring meat, fish, chicken, and vegetarian entrees.

The owner/chef, Ransom Stewart, didn't have any professional training as a chef, but created delicious dishes that received high marks from critics and diners. He was the media darling on the Atlanta culinary scene—an attorney who'd left a successful career in civil litigation to open a restaurant.

His wife, Sophie, had been bringing her vehicle to

Taylor Automotive & Repair for years. She personally greeted Ezekiel and Ronnie the moment they stepped into the restaurant and pulled them each into a boisterous hug.

"Welcome!" Her golden skin glowed under the ambient lighting. Curly hair in a neat bundle at her nape, she smiled her wide smile at them.

Ezekiel eyed her loose-fitting dress. "Wait a minute now. Don't tell me that husband of yours has already knocked you up."

"Daddy..." Ronnie covered her face in embarrassment, but Sophie laughed, her skin and eyes glowing.

"Yes, he has, Mr. Taylor. I'm going to be a mommy before too long."

"Congratulations," Ronnie said.

"Thank you. Okay, you two, follow me. I'm giving you the star treatment. I placed you in a private room upstairs."

The private room was decorated with oil paintings depicting farm life, an ode to the farm-to-table philosophy of the restaurant. The room Sophie chose contained a table that accommodated twelve, and guests already sat at the table: three of the school's top graduates—two young men and one young woman—three teachers, the dean, and two other administrators.

"Order anything you like," the dean said, adjusting his glasses.

"Oh, I don't know if I should do that," Ezekiel said. He sat at the head of the table and picked up the menu.

"We insist." One of the other administrators leaned in his direction. Ronnie wondered how long she'd been sitting there, since she already had what looked like an apple martini in front of her. "It's your night."

Ezekiel chuckled and said, "All right, then."

"The rib eye steak is very popular, and I also highly recommend any of the vegetable dishes," Sophie said. "I'll leave you all in Nancy's very capable hands. She'll take good care of you."

She left the room and the waitress, Nancy, took their orders. They started with appetizers and drinks, and when Nancy came back a second time with those items, they placed orders for the entrees. Ronnie ordered the rib eye with sautéed spinach and scalloped potatoes. Her father ordered the rib eye as well, but paired it with mashed potatoes and steamed vegetables.

Time passed quickly, and halfway through the dinner conversation, the female student beside her turned to Ronnie and asked, "Is it hard for you, being a woman in this field?"

Her name was Rachel, and she couldn't be more than nineteen or twenty. She spoke in a quiet undertone, obviously not wishing anyone else at the table to hear the question. Despite being one of the top students at the school, doubt clouded her eyes.

Ronnie considered the question before answering. She wanted to encourage, not discourage the young woman, so she chose her words carefully.

"I haven't had many problems, but I have experienced pushback and skepticism from ignorant people," she replied, keeping her voice equally low. "Unfortunately, our industry has a terrible reputation. But for the most part, customers are polite and easy to work with if you know what you're doing. Speak confidently and treat them fairly and with integrity. As for the male mechanics, I worked with my dad for years before I took over the shop, so the men knew and respected me. Now that I'm their boss, they *really* respect me."

Rachel smiled. "I just wonder how easy it will be for me to find a job."

"Opportunities for women are better than they used to be, but you can't be just as good as the men—you have to be better to get the same amount of respect. Once you gain their respect, they'll have your back."

Rachel nodded. "I know what you mean. When I first started classes, the guys gave me a hard time. They didn't want to work on projects with me, and excluded me from activities outside of the classroom. For months I ate lunch by myself. But once I proved I could do the work, they stopped shutting me out. It was slow at first, but eventually I earned their respect." She smiled tentatively.

"Work on getting a couple of ASE certifications once you're eligible," Ronnie advised.

"I will."

They rejoined the conversation at the table, where wine flowed freely among the adults. When Ronnie saw everyone was almost finished with their meals, she called over the waitress.

"Go ahead and bring everything up," she whispered.

The young woman nodded and took off.

An additional surprise awaited her father. A very nice glass plaque, a cake with "Thank you" on top of it, and gifts had been brought to the restaurant earlier. Minutes later, Nancy and two other servers arrived carrying all the items. "Surprise!" they said.

They set the cake in front of her father and piled the gifts on top of the table in front of him.

Everyone at the table clapped and cheered.

"What's all this?" Ezekiel said, his eyes watery.

The head of the automotive program spoke. "We want you to know how much we appreciate everything you do for the students. Thank you so much for the time you spend sharing your knowledge. You enrich our lives, and the program is so much better for having you a part of it."

They all clapped again, and Ronnie patted her father's hand.

Ezekiel sat quietly for a minute, and the group waited while he gathered his composure. When he could finally speak, he lifted his watery gaze and spoke with a little tremor in his voice. "I volunteer because I love it. Love those kids and love the work I did for most of my life. I never expected to be rewarded. Thank you." More clapping, and then Nancy cut the cake and shared the pieces to all the guests at the table.

****

At the end of the evening, with the help of Nancy and another server, Ronnie and Ezekiel carried all the gifts and the leftover cake to the car. Her father talked almost nonstop, and she let him continue uninterrupted, which gave her time to think about Diego. Her concern for his mental state reemerged on the drive home.

What was he doing? Was he okay tonight of all nights—when the memories of his deceased daughter were sure to plague his thoughts?

At home, she helped her father take his gifts

upstairs and then sat on the foot of the bed and chatted with him. She thought she'd done a good job of engaging, but her father squeezed her hand.

"You're not even here with me, nugget."

"I'm sorry. I'm just worried about Diego," she admitted.

"You should check on him. I'm sure he'd appreciate that." Her father patted her hand.

"You're right. I'll go over there and make sure he's okay."

"Good idea."

"I'm proud of you. Get some rest." She rose from the bed and kissed her father on the forehead. "Don't wait up. I'll probably stay over."

"All right. Drive safely."

Chapter Twenty-three

Ronnie parked and sat for a few minutes. There were no lights on in Diego's house. If he was already asleep, she didn't want to wake him. Of course, he could be out. Perhaps he simply didn't want to spend the evening with her and her father, and might be with friends or gone to see Tomas, as he'd done once before.

She decided to try to reach him, and if he didn't come to the door, she'd leave him a note so he at least knew he was on her mind.

Ronnie rang the doorbell and waited. A dog barked nearby, and she heard the sound of a train roaring over the tracks a mile or so from the subdivision.

She rang the bell again and waited.

Still nothing.

She returned to the truck, took a napkin from the glove compartment, and found a pen under the driver's seat. She was about to write Diego a note when a light came on inside the house.

He *was* home.

Ronnie crushed the paper in her hand and arrived at the door just as it was opened—but not by Diego.

Her stomach dropped and lips parted in quiet shock.

A woman stood in the doorway—the Cristina Milian lookalike from the photos on the wall—wearing one of Diego's sleeveless undershirts. The same item of clothing Ronnie enjoyed lounging in when she stayed with him. Only she'd never filled out the shirts in the same way.

She couldn't be sure the woman wore anything else under it. Certainly not a bra, because the outlines of her ample breasts were clearly visible through the thin material. The hem fell past her curvaceous hips, and she was barefoot, looking completely at ease.

This was the "something" that had suddenly come up, forcing Diego to cancel plans scheduled weeks ago. This woman, his ex, who looked impossibly more beautiful in person, with her long, dark hair in a tousled mess. Like a woman who'd just rolled out of bed.

Nausea clawed up Ronnie's throat. She was going to be sick. Not here. Not now. Not in front of this woman.

"Can I help you?" She appeared to be a little unsteady on her feet, and gripped the door.

"I..." Ronnie croaked. She didn't know what to say.

She couldn't help. No one could. If she hadn't come here tonight, unannounced, tomorrow Diego could have concocted a perfectly reasonable explanation for cancelling on dinner, and she wouldn't have known any different.

Lying to her. Cheating on her. Just like Leonard.

Anger and hurt burned her chest. Men were all the same. Said they wanted one type, but always went for the feminine, girly ones. And who better to fall back into bed with than an ex, with whom you shared a bond?

"No, you can't help me."

The woman looked at her strangely, confusion wrinkling her brow. Then the frown cleared, and for a moment she saw clarity in the other woman's eyes. A smile—more like a smirk—hovered around her lips before she closed the door.

Drawing a tremulous breath, Ronnie backed away. At the same time, a round of headlights flashed across the house. Turning quickly, she saw Diego's black truck pull up beside hers.

No. She couldn't see him now.

He hopped out holding a plastic sack in hand and his gaze swung between her and the door. He quickly assessed the situation. "Veronica, wait."

She raced toward her vehicle to evade him, but he caught her around the waist with one hand.

"Let go of me!" she screeched.

"I can explain," he growled close to her ear.

"I don't want to hear it."

She elbow-jabbed him in the ribs and he grunted, loosening his hold enough for her to twist free.

"You're a liar," she spat. Her hands transformed into angry fists, agony ripping through her veins, her skin, her heart.

"I didn't lie." He spoke calmly and set the groceries or whatever the hell he held in the bag on the cement and lifted a placating hand toward her.

"Something came up?"

"I can explain, if you let me."

"Explain? There's nothing to explain." Her voice trembled with embarrassment and hurt. "I get it, okay? She's pretty and sexy and has a terrific body."

"You're pretty. You're sexy. You have a terrific body."

"And after all, you have history. She may have cheated on you, but you obviously still care. It's hard to turn off those emotions."

"Don't tell me what I feel," Diego ground out. Even in the dark she clearly saw the hardening of his jaw and the flash of irritation in his eyes.

"Are you denying it?" Ronnie asked.

"Of course! She's my ex. *Ex*. For a reason."

"Then what is she doing here? She hardly had any clothes on. Only your shirt."

He grimaced. "She came over, hurting, drunk. I couldn't turn her away. Not tonight of all nights."

"How very kind of you."

"She's been resting."

"In your bed?" Ronnie asked snidely.

"I know how this looks, which is why I didn't tell you over the phone. The reason she had my shirt on was because she threw up on her clothes, and I gave her something to wear. *Nothing happened.*"

Ronnie shook her head. "I wish I could believe you, but I've been here before."

"You're not being fair, Veronica."

"You know what I don't get? You pursued me. For a whole year. I didn't want to have anything to do with you because I knew it was too good to be true. And here you are, proving me right." Unshed tears stung her eyes.

One of the Guys

She had been perfectly fine by herself—alone, but happy. A state not easily achieved after the heartbreak she suffered from Leonard. But mentally she had arrived at a place where she accepted her single status. Until Diego changed her mind. Until he made her have feelings long ago suppressed and provoked emotions she purposely turned off.

"You're wrong. I wanted to be there tonight. I wanted to celebrate with you and your father. I wanted to get my mind off of the significance of today's date." He ran a hand through his hair. "You have to believe me."

"No, I don't. I trust my eyes. Not your empty words. Go back inside and play house with your ex and leave me the hell alone."

She rushed to her vehicle and hopped in.

She flicked on the headlights and he stayed right there, illuminated and unmoved. Ronnie cranked the engine and backed out with a squeal of tires. Seconds later she roared out of the subdivision, on the way home.

The tears she'd dared not let fall in front of Diego tumbled from her eyes. And to think she'd come over there out of concern. She swiped tears from her eyes, falling into a vortex of emotions.

Hating him. Loving him. Hating herself for loving him.

Chapter Twenty-four

Ronnie lay face down on her pillow. She didn't know the time. Maybe late morning or early afternoon. Either way, she didn't care. She had no intention of leaving the house today or tomorrow. Maybe ever.

Good grief, she'd turned into such an emotional drama queen.

The doorbell rang, and she rolled onto her back. After crying all night, her puffy eyes burned. She pulled the pillow over her face to protect her eyes from the sun's glare.

The doorbell rang again.

Who could that be? And where was her father?

She rolled out of bed and peeped out the window. Diego's truck sat in the driveway. Her heart constricted painfully. He wasn't in it, though. He must be standing at the door, hidden by the eaves.

She sagged against the sill. His betrayal cut deep. She didn't want to see him. Shouldn't want to.

She heard movement downstairs and tiptoed across the floor to crack the bedroom door open.

"What do you want?" her father asked in an extra-gruff voice.

She smiled at his rudeness and appreciated the support of her protective Papa Bear. He liked Diego and was almost as hurt and disappointed as she was when she burst into his room last night and told him what she discovered when she went to his house.

"Good morning, Mr. Taylor," Diego said.

"Don't you good morning me," her father snapped. "I'm very disappointed in you. Whatever you have to say, you can keep it to yourself. No amount of apologizing is going to fix what you've done. You hurt my daughter."

"She misunderstood what she saw."

"Anything else?"

Conversation paused for a moment, and Ronnie strained to hear. Were they having a staring contest?

Diego spoke quietly, and then her father asked in a sharp voice, "What's that?"

"Something for her."

"I doubt Ronnie will want anything from you."

"She'll want this."

"I doubt it, but all right. I'll let Ronnie decide what she wants to do."

"Thank you. And would you tell her if she wants to talk, I'm home. By myself."

"By yourself? Quite the change from last night," Ezekiel said.

The door slammed closed and Ronnie crossed the room and went back to bed. She pulled the covers up to her waist and waited for her father. He came up shortly and knocked on the door.

"Come in."

When he came in, she expected to see flowers or balloons or some kind of apologetic gift. Instead, he dropped a slick red folder onto the bedspread.

"What's that?"

"Diego left that for you."

Ronnie sat up and opened the folder.

"He looked pitiful," Ezekiel said. "You wouldn't know the two of you just argued last night. He looked like he hasn't slept in days."

"You're not getting soft on me are you?" Ronnie asked.

"Not at all. But are you sure about him?"

"I know what I saw."

"All right, then. Anybody hurt my baby, they hurt me too." He patted an ankle under the bedspread.

She could always count on her father, the one man she could trust.

"You getting out of bed anytime soon?" he asked.

"In a little bit," Ronnie answered, distracted by the folder and the contents.

"Okay, whenever you're ready, I'll take you to breakfast."

"The breakfast buffet?" she asked hopefully.

Going to breakfast was one of the things they liked to do, and they often went to the same place, which offered delicious servings of ham, cheese grits, scrambled eggs, toast, and pancakes. They'd been going there since she was a little girl, and right now she felt young and vulnerable like a little girl. Comfort food and her father's nurturing nature offered the perfect salve for her emotional bruises.

"Is there any place else for breakfast?" He grinned.

"Not at all."

After her father left the room, Ronnie read the contents of the package, a professional and detailed marketing plan. Did Diego pay someone to do this?

Her heart raced triple time as she reviewed the extensive report tailored specifically for Taylor Automotive & Repair. She reviewed the colorful graphs and charts and skimmed the market analysis of potential customers available in the surrounding area. What most intrigued Ronnie was the recommendation to focus on women customers.

She turned to the next page, which detailed a wonderful idea of doing community outreach through an automotive clinic for women. The clinic would teach the basics of car maintenance to educate female drivers, but serve as a funnel to establish trust and future business.

Why hadn't she thought of this herself? It was a brilliant idea.

Ronnie rolled out of bed and rushed to the window. Diego had already left, of course. She picked up the phone and dialed his number, but it rolled to voicemail. She should probably thank him in person, anyway.

In the bathroom, she splashed cool water on her face, curling her lip at her swollen eyes, but shrugged since there was nothing she could do about them. Dressing quickly, she donned a lime-green shirt and a denim skirt, absolutely not wearing a skirt because Diego liked her legs.

She scooped up the package from the bed, and rushed down the stairs.

Her father came down the hall, his eyes wide and startled. "Where you going in such a hurry? What about breakfast?"

"I need a rain check. This"—she held up the package—"is a marketing plan on how we can expand Taylor Automotive."

"Diego did that?" her father asked.

"Maybe he paid someone. I don't know. But I'm going to thank him."

"Thank him?"

"Yes. I…couldn't get him on the phone."

"Uh-huh. Good luck, nugget."

Ronnie bit her lip. "I'm only going to thank him."

"Okay," her father said, a gleam in his eyes.

Ronnie arrived at Diego's and then second-guessed herself. Dread ate at the insides of her stomach. Maybe she should have left a message instead of coming over.

The front door opened and Diego stood there in a pair of jeans and no shirt.

Crap. Now she couldn't leave.

She exited the vehicle and made her way slowly to the door on unsteady legs. Stopping a few feet away, she hugged the folder to her chest. "Hey."

"Hey." His face appeared drawn, and her father was right—he looked like someone who hadn't slept in days. Despite the tiredness, he was as handsome as ever. A dusting of bristles on his face, and his hair tousled and uncombed. She wanted to launch into his arms.

"Are you alone? I—"

His mouth tightened.

She started again. "Can I come in?"

He stepped aside and she walked into the living room. Bonkers lounged in her favorite spot on the arm of the sofa, licking her paw. She watched Ronnie with suspicious eyes, her tail swishing up and down, the way a human would impatiently tap their fingers.

"I read the report," Ronnie said.

"What did you think?" A tuft of dark hair peeked out from the top of his low-slung jeans, distracting her.

"It's great. How much do I owe you?"

"Nothing. Talia works at a marketing firm and prepared it as a favor to me." He spoke in a dull, flat voice.

"Wow, that's some favor. She put in a lot of work, or so it seems. You're sure there isn't something I could do? Maybe offer free service or something?" She smiled, lips trembling with the effort to remain cool.

"You don't have to do that. She's family."

Ronnie hugged the report tighter. There was nothing more to say. She should leave, but couldn't.

"You only came by to thank me?"

She lifted her gaze and saw pain in his eyes. But she felt pain, too. Deep, ugly pain that shredded her insides and made her feel like a fool.

"I'm angry at you," she said quietly.

"If you let me explain—"

"I know all the stories, I know the game. I've been on the inside."

"So I'm just like every other man, is that it? Is that fair? We hit a snag and you bail?"

"Snag? Is that what you call what you did?" She wanted to scream.

"I didn't *do* anything!" he shot back. A vein pulsed in his forehead.

"Yes, you did!" Her arm muscles quivered. Tension choked her. "You pursued me for a year, and you gave me hope. Hope that you liked me for *me*.

With all my rough edges. I didn't have to pretend to be someone else—something else. You made me believe that I was fine the way I was, whether I was Veronica, or whether I was Ronnie." She took a quivering breath. "And then you took back the hope and the love and stomped on me. On us."

"I never took anything back, *mami*," he said.

"Your ex was here, half-naked in your house..." She choked on the words.

"What you saw was me helping someone who once meant a lot to me. Nothing more."

She wanted to believe him. Dare she? His eyes looked so sincere. The words sounded heartfelt.

"Loisa and I have history, but I don't love her. I love you. I meant the words when I said them before, and I mean them now."

He came closer, and the muscles in her shoulders tightened in protective tension.

"I did not cheat on you with my ex. Memorial Day weekend, you asked me to trust you. What about you? Can you trust me, Veronica?"

He was the only person who called her that. The only man who treated her with such care and consideration. With him she could be vulnerable, without feeling weak. She could be strong and still reach for him, and his steady hand would be there, at her elbow, or supporting her back.

"Can you trust me?" he asked again. "Trust us?"

He stood right in front of her, and Ronnie squeezed her eyes tight. She leaned into him, perilously close to tears.

Diego enveloped her in his arms, and she rested against his warm chest. He rubbed up and down her back, and she melted—simply melted against him.

He kissed the top of her head, and she sighed contentedly.

"Yes. I trust you," Ronnie whispered.

Chapter Twenty-five

Phone to her ear, Ronnie peered into the kitchen, where Tomas and his crew worked, the sound of power tools and pounding hammers almost constant two days into the renovations.

Thanks to the advice from Tomas's wife Talia, business had picked up at Taylor Automotive & Repair. The auto clinic was a success, and the free publicity from a feature on the evening news created an avalanche of interest. So much so Ronnie had hired on the two part-time technicians as full-timers and could now afford to remodel the kitchen.

She strolled to the sunken living room and plopped onto the sofa next to Diego. His fingers moved quickly over the phone as he replied to a text.

Ronnie draped her leg over his and continued the conversation with her father. "I have great news."

He and Miss Loretta had married a month ago in a small ceremony in the backyard, officiated by their church pastor. Seventy-five friends and family attended, including Jacob and Buck from the barbershop, and Anika and her mother.

Her father and Miss Loretta were on their honeymoon—a two-week getaway in Hilton Head.

"What's the news?" her father asked.

Ronnie clearly heard the sound of the Atlantic Ocean through the phone.

"The association gave our yard an honorary mention in the beautification awards."

Red, yellow, and purple flowers added eye-popping color to the landscape, and a white sign with black letters sat at the edge of the lawn, announcing the honor to the entire neighborhood.

"It's your yard now."

He had partially moved into Miss Loretta's home. He planned to do a full move-in when they returned from their honeymoon, but had already signed over his house to Ronnie. Thanks to her father, she was now a homeowner and business owner.

"You and Diego did all the work," Ronnie pointed out.

Diego raised his head when she said his name and then went back to texting.

"Reynolds took the title again, I take it," Ezekiel said.

"Yes."

Her father grunted. "I'm starting to think the competition is rigged. Talk to Diego about new ideas. Next year I want you to win top prize."

Ronnie laughed at his newfound competitive streak. Until Diego, he'd never expressed interest in the awards. "Daddy, I'm not worried about that."

"Talk to Diego," he said again.

Ronnie rolled her eyes. "Okay, whatever. I'll talk

to him about it. I'll let you go so you can soak up some more sun."

"All right, nugget. We'll see you in ten days. What's that?" She heard muffled speaking, as if he'd covered the phone. Then, "Loretta said hello."

"Tell her I said hello back. Talk to you later. Love you."

"Love you, too."

Ronnie rested her head against Diego's arm. "What's on the agenda for today?" she asked. They'd both taken the day off, the first Saturday in a long time.

"Actually, I need to discuss something with you," he said.

"What?" She lifted her head to look at him.

She'd come to know his moods very well. At the moment, he wore that cute, mischievous look he sometimes did when he had an idea he wanted to share with her. The same look came over his face whenever he wanted her to try something new in the bedroom. She wondered if that was what he had in mind.

Last time she saw that look, she'd wound up with a particularly powerful orgasm after letting him restrain her with one of his ties. The spontaneity of their sex life was one of the many things she enjoyed about being with him.

"You know I play basketball at the gym."

"And yet you suck so bad."

He tugged her ear.

"Stop." She slapped away his hand.

"Listen up." Diego tugged her ear again, and Ronnie winced. "As I was saying, you know I usually play on Saturday afternoon and kick ass." He waited for her to object, and when she didn't, continued. "We have a competition going with another team, but a member of our team has to cancel."

"Okay, I'll bite. How do you plan to get around being one man short?"

The mischievous smile turned sly. "You."

"Hmm. Is money involved?" Ronnie asked.

"Do Cubans do it better?"

Ronnie sighed. "Yes, Cubans do it better."

"Say it with more conviction."

"You know what…"

"You have something smart to say?" He lifted his hand like a claw and flexed his fingers, threatening her with a bout of tickles.

"Cubans are the greatest," Ronnie said woodenly. "They definitely do it better."

"We'll have to work on your delivery," Diego said. "Anyway, are you game?"

"Is my name Ronnie Taylor, Queen of the Basketball Court?" Ronnie responded with a saucy smile.

He grinned, all white teeth and gorgeous lips. "I don't know about all that, but I'm ready to whoop some ass."

****

That afternoon, Ronnie and Diego showed up at the gym, but when his teammates learned that Ronnie would be taking the place of their fourth member, their shoulders sagged in defeat.

"Come on, man. No offense, but you brought your lady in here to replace Ty?" The teammate, a light-skinned black male with a white sweatband around his head, stared in disbelief at Ronnie.

She stood to the side, stretching in preparation of

the game, and could hear everything they said. Of course, she didn't get the impression they *didn't* want her to hear.

"She's better than all of us. Trust me," Diego said. All three of them sent their gazes in her direction, and Ronnie continued loosening her limbs, bending from side to side in a lateral stretch.

"Unless she's Lisa Leslie reincarnated, I'm not buying it," the other team member said. He looked biracial, black and Asian.

"Hey!" A member from the opposite team yelled across the court and pointed at Ronnie. "We playing ball, or we doing tai chi all day? Cause I came to play ball."

Ronnie smirked at the remark and her gaze met Diego's.

"Are you ready?" he asked.

"I'm always ready." She couldn't wait to make those suckers feel her wrath.

The game was a massacre. Ronnie was small and fast and they never saw her coming. She stole the ball and zipped between them for layups. By the time they figured out they needed to keep her from approaching the goal, she changed tactics and only shot three-pointers. They never stood a chance.

At the end of the game, their opponents came over and shook her hand.

"I got mad respect for you," one of the guys said, giving her a fist bump.

"We have to go celebrate," Diego's light-skinned teammate said. "Drinks on me."

"Nah." Diego pulled Ronnie to his side. "We're going home."

"You sure?" his other teammate said. "You know

this cheap bastard never pays for anything, so we might as well take advantage."

Diego chuckled. "We're good, thanks."

They watched them walk away. "I owe you," Diego said.

"Yeah, you do."

"I'll go get my gym bag and then we can leave."

He jogged off toward the bleachers.

"Ronnie." A voice from the past called her name from nearby.

She blinked. Once. Twice.

Leonard, her ex. At least two years had passed since she heard news about him, and four since she'd seen him. Yet here he was, in the flesh. He always kept his body in good shape, and an Atlanta Hawks jersey displayed his thick, muscular arms.

"Hi."

"How are you?" The corners of his eyes crinkled into a smile. He actually looked pleased to see her. "Still working at your dad's shop?"

"My dad retired. I run it now," Ronnie answered proudly.

"Congratulations." Admiration filled his eyes and voice. "Dahlia came to watch me play. She's sitting over there." He indicated the location with a nod toward the bleachers on the opposite side of the gymnasium.

Dahlia looked ready to go out on a night on the town instead of a casual afternoon watching her boyfriend play ball. She wore a short-sleeved maxi dress with long necklaces around her neck, and matching earrings. Her hair was cut in a chic bob, combed without a hair out of place.

Leonard cleared his throat. "I don't know if you

heard, but we got married last year."

There was a time when hearing that would have destroyed her, but she felt nothing now. Not even a twinge.

"I'm happy to hear it," Ronnie said and, to her surprise, realized she meant it. She used to wish all manner of harm and injury to befall Leonard, but she harbored no ill will toward him—not anymore. She'd grown a lot, and finding love mellowed her.

"I better go. My boyfriend's waiting for me." She indicated Diego over at the bleachers, with the gym bag over his shoulders, watching the exchange.

"Damn. I'm not gay, but that's a nice-looking dude."

Ronnie laughed. "He's not just good-looking—he's nice, too."

Leonard scratched the back of his head. "I always felt guilty about the way things ended between us and hoped you met someone."

"There's no need for you to feel guilty. Besides, I'm not in the same place I was four years ago."

"I can tell. You're...different." He shrugged. "I don't know how to explain it."

"I'm happy," Ronnie said simply.

"I understand. The right person can really make a difference."

"Yes, and on that note, I'm really going to leave. Take care, and although you probably don't need it, good luck with your game." Ronnie walked away.

"Thanks. And you played your ass off. Good game."

She didn't know he'd been there the entire time and seen her play. "I know."

Leonard chuckled and she strutted over to Diego,

an extra bounce in her step. He slipped an arm around her shoulder and they walked toward the exit together.

"Why didn't you come over?" Ronnie asked, threading her fingers through his hand on her shoulder.

"Had a feeling you needed to talk to him alone. Was I right?"

"Yes."

"Who is he?"

"Leonard." A while back, she told him all about the man who broke her heart, and she and Diego commiserated over being cheated on and how the experience tarnished their view of relationships.

She leaned on him as they crossed the gym to the double doors.

"What did he have to say?"

"Nothing much. He complimented me on the game and said I seemed different."

"Really? What did you say?"

Ronnie smiled up at him. "I told him I was happy."

More Stories by Delaney Diamond

Love Unexpected series
The Blind Date
The Wrong Man
An Unexpected Attraction
The Right Time
One of the Guys
That Time in Venice (coming soon)

Johnson Family series
Unforgettable
Perfect
Just Friends
The Rules
Good Behavior (coming soon)

Hot Latin Men series
The Arrangement
Fight for Love
Private Acts
The Ultimate Merger
Second Chances
More Than a Mistress (coming soon)
Hot Latin Men: Vol. I (print anthology)
Hot Latin Men: Vol. II (print anthology)

Hawthorne Family series
The Temptation of a Good Man
A Hard Man to Love
Here Comes Trouble
For Better or Worse
Hawthorne Family Series: Vol. I (print anthology)
Hawthorne Family Series: Vol. II (print anthology)

Bailar series (sweet/clean romance)
Worth Waiting For

Stand Alones
Still in Love
Subordinate Position
Heartbreak in Rio (part of Endless summer Nights)

Free Stories
www.delaneydiamond.com

About the Author

Delaney Diamond is the USA Today Bestselling Author of sweet, sensual, passionate romance novels. Originally from the U.S. Virgin Islands, she now lives in Atlanta, Georgia. She reads romance novels, mysteries, thrillers, and a fair amount of nonfiction. When she's not busy reading or writing, she's in the kitchen trying out new recipes, dining at one of her favorite restaurants, or traveling to an interesting locale. She speaks fluent conversational French and can get by in Spanish.

Enjoy free reads and the first chapter of all her novels on her website. Join her e-mail mailing list to get sneak peeks, notices of sale prices, and find out about new releases.

www.delaneydiamond.com

Made in the USA
Lexington, KY
29 June 2016